CONTENTS

SPIC-O-RAMA

© Jeff Vespa

About the Author

JOHN LEGUIZAMO was born in Bogota, Colombia, in 1964. When he was four, his family immigrated to the United States, where they settled in Queens, New York. He began his career as a standup comedian in various New York clubs, and has gone on to critically acclaimed performances in film, in television, and on Broadway. He has two children and lives in New York.

THE WORKS OF

JOHN LEGUIZAMO

AN ecco BOOK

HARPER

NEW YORK • LONDON • TORONTO • SYDNEY

FREAK
SPIC-O-RAMA
MAMBO MOUTH
AND SEXAHOLIX

John Leguizamo

HARPER

FIRST EDITION

Designed by Cassandra J. Pappas

Library of Congress Cataloging-in-Publication data is available upon
request.

ISBN: 978-0-06-052070-0

08 09 10 11 12 DIX/RRD 10 9 8 7 6 5 4 3 2 1

MAMBO MOUTH

SEXAHOLIX

FREAK

A SEMI-DEMI-PSEUDO

AUTOBIOGRAPHY

JOHN LEGUIZAMO

WITH DAVID BAR KATZ

I t was the spring of '95 and John and I had just come off of a year and a half of working on "House of Buggin'." We were sitting around my apartment when John innocently suggested that we do a stand-up comedy show, some kind of John Leguizamo-in-Concert-Richard-Pryoresque-Extravaganza that would be different from John's previous shows in that it wouldn't be overtly theatrical. John then said it would be "fun," as though it would be a break for us.

But as soon as the writing began, something horrible happened: real emotion raised its ugly head. Our writing sessions, which had initially just been made up of riffing on jokes, were turning into in-depth psychoanalytic sessions. In my little office we were delving into all the love, sickness, and horror that are the grist of an ethnic person's life, and we were still just on me. My family life had exactly paralleled John's in every way (other than being Jewish, going to prep school, and not knowing how to pronounce "pollo"), so I had an intimate understanding of his emotional life: we both adored our grandmothers, were both Momma's boys, and both had a love/hate relationship with our fathers—we loved them; they hated us.

The first thing people always ask me after they see the show is, "Did it all really happen to John, is it all true?" (The exception being my mother who is now convinced that *my* father had me de-flowered at a Kentucky Fried Chicken.) To answer the truth question, I'll break down a couple of scenes in the play to give the reader an "insider's view."

There is a scene where John throws his own shit while playing in the pool at a Jewish resort. Now, John really did go to a Jewish resort as a child, though he did not actually throw shit there. But because he has thrown his own shit at other times in his life, I consider the story true.

There's also a scene where John is hit so hard he dies—his soul leaves his body and ascends to heaven. Now, it is true that John has been hit (many times, actually). It is also true that his soul has left his body, but rather than ascending to heaven, as we've depicted it in *Freak*, his soul plunged down into a burning pit until it reached Hades, where it was greeted by Satan. I thought it best to edit this a bit. We don't want to scare the kids.

So there you have it; *Freak*, 100% kind-of-true.*

—DAVID BAR KATZ,
Lower East Side, June 19, 1997

---

*Or, as our lawyers insist we put it, the characters in *Freak* are wildly exaggerated for comic effect and bear little or no resemblance to actual people.

The following text is based on the stage show "Freak—A Semi-Demi-Quasi-Pseudo Autobiography." The show was written to be performed but has been adapted here to be a joyous read. Because we are right now in the midst of the show's developmental process, this version represents where the show is at this exact moment, June 19, 1997. It will be different tomorrow and even more different the day after. We only tell you this because if you try to read along with the book to a performance, you're gonna get really confused.

—JOHN LEGUIZAMO & DAVID BAR KATZ

MEETING WOMB

I've changed my parents' names to Fausto and Lala, to protect the innocent, namely me. I was born in Latin America, cause my moms was there. And when I was born, my moms was in labor for forty-eight hours, but she didn't care because she was enthralled with the miracle of creating life. "Ow! Desgraciado, get this parasite out of me! Get it out of me now!! Coño."

And my dad's going, "If I had a nickel for every time I heard that."

The doctor was also a little anxious. "Push! Ms. Liquidzamo, Ms. Legs and amo, leg of lamb . . . Just push ma'am!"

"With what, cabron! With what?!!"

And Dad says, "I'm paying you, doctor! Why don't you pull!?"

"I am pulling! He's a stubborn little fuck."

"Then leave him in there. Get up, woman, we're leaving."

"But Fausto, he's half out."

"So wear something loose. Come on, woman."

So they walked out and my first view of the world was upside down and between my moms' legs. And they wonder why I have problems.

*

My parents left Latin America during the big plantain famine of the late sixties, and when they arrived in New York City they had such thick accents they couldn't even understand each other. My moms got all her English from watching television. "Fausto, chock full of nuts is the heavenly coffee, they're creepy and they're cookie, that . . . that . . . that's all folks!"

"Woman, what the hell did you just say?"

"How should I know? I'm speaking English."

At the airport, the nice, very white, very southern customs officer comes over to help. "Come now, strip naked! Deep cavity search time. Last week we found five Nicaraguans inside one of you people."

He starts searching my moms.

"OOhh, his hands are cold. Fausto, why don't you touch me like this?"

"Cause I'm not looking for anything. Hey, Mr. Officer, if we're being searched, why are you naked?"

"Shut up and bend over!"

He puts on a rubber glove and welcomes my dad to America.

"No, mister, please no! ow, ow, ow!" Then my dad started singing, "America America God shed his grace on thee."

*

The shuttle from the airport said "Miserable and Huddled Masses" and my pops is like, "This is our bus," so we jumped on and ended up in the present-day Ellis Island—Jackson Heights, Queens. Our tenement building was like the modern Tower of Babel. When I walked through the streets I'd see every ethnicity under the sun. The Hindi guy would be like, "You want curry candy? It burn the shit out of your buttocks. Ring of fire." Then the Jamaican rasta, "You people multiply like roaches go back, blood clots, batty fufu, chatty chatty. Tinga linga ling hear the money ring. Buyaca buyaca." And the Korean newsstand guy, "This is not a library, little punks. You buy magazine or kick your ass."

*

My parents worked twenty-eight hours a day, fourteen days a week. I'm not bad at math; it's just that Latin people have to make the most of their time. But my pops always took time out of his busy schedule to tell us his own version of an American bedtime story. "Once upon a time there was a Little Red Riding Hood and she went into the woods and got a green card and lived happily ever after. Now shut the fuck up and go to sleep!"

*

Of course, we Latin guys are always treated like little kings by our moms, and that's where we get that macho shit going to the max. And my moms would fill my head with it even when I was a baby in my high chair getting fed.

"You, you are the center of the universe. You are all things to me. Don't be tan estupid. Let the world come to you. Fuck everyone else, mijo, you are the prize—ah-ah, learn to share!" (Moms couldn't resist my strained carrots.)

"And remember, mijo, any woman that fucks you will probably fuck somebody else, okay? And you don't want to marry a whore! Cause no woman's good enough for my little Latin King."

At this point she would usually break down. I'd be like, "What's a whore, mommy?"

Slap! Right across my innocent chubby little face.

"Don't you ever repeat back to me what I say to you in the after-noons when I've been drinking a little."

*

Now, I have a theory that everybody's got a nice grandmother and a mean, evil, insane one. And I was always afraid that if they ever touched, their converse powers would mutually annihilate each other. I was eight when I first learned which was which. I was at a family barbecue with forty or fifty of my cousins carpooling on one hibachi. And my gramps was there on his life support system. We were keeping him alive against his will. Because my pops wanted him to live long enough so he would suffer what he had made my pops suffer. He would always motion me over, then he'd be like . . . "Pull the plug. No one's looking, John, pull the plug!"

"But, abuelito, you know I'm not supposed to touch your iron lung . . ."

"Just do it. Just do it. Mother@#$%*!"

"Okay, Goodbye, Gramps."

I'd give him a kiss, then pull the plug. But my dad had an un-canny ability to sense my grandfather escaping. He'd rush over just in time . . . "Hey, you know you're not supposed to put your grandfa-ther out of his misery."

Then he'd plug him back in. "Nice try, old man."

I always tried to avoid my cousins Speedy and Boulevard, cause the games they played with the police by day, they reenacted on me by weekend. "Johnny, ven, mira, ven, quiero hablar contigo. Let's play po-lice brutality. I'm a cop and tu eres un criminal. Aqui, take this gun!"

And they would toss a gun into my hand.

"I don't wanna play!" I'd scream. But it would be too late.

"Take him down, he's got a gun." Then they would jump on me and kick me and sing, "We're playing with Johnito, Johnito."

You might know my cousin Speedy—he's that shirtless Latin guy that you see on "Cops" each week. So I ran up to one of my grams for comfort. And my grandmother would cradle my little cherub face in her hands and say, "Ay, pobrecito, nenito consentido, what are you, a little girl? Come here, come here, let me put a dress on you, you little pussy!"

"I am what I eat." Grams' hand came flying up from South America, across the Bronx, down Spanish Harlem, and smacked me in the face. "Ow! I read that somewhere. I hope your Miracle Ear breaks, you scrotum-faced old . . ."

"What did you say?" Grams hissed. "Like I care what a little fag thinks of me. Oh, look everyone, look at my little granddaughter. Speedy, Boulevard, come here, come here. I'll hold her down while you kick her ass."

And she was the *nice* Grandma. So then I ran up to my other grams, hoping for comfort, my midget Grama Dulce, which is Spanish for candy, cause her fingers were always sticky even though she never ate any candy. She was a Seventh-Day Adventist and had powerful beliefs, like, *The Exorcist* was actually a documentary, and that since there were no Latin people in *Star Trek* it was proof they weren't planning on having us around for the future. Her opinions got especially strong after she'd tip back a few fifths of holy water. Then she'd slip into this scary other voice and say things like, "If you (hiccup) levitate any furniture in my house or spit green puke on my clothes, I'm going to slap the shit out of you. And that goes for all one—two—of you."

"But Grama Dulce, I know it's not you, it's the alcohol talking," I'd insist.

"Lies! Lies!" she'd scream *(hiccup)*. "You're the Prince of Lies. I know who you are, Lucifer. Leave the body of my grandson, demon!" Then she'd grab me and say, "Hold still. I'm going to drive your evil spirit away! Lord bless this Jack Daniel's." And she'd toss her drink in my face.

"It burns. My eyes. It burns," I'd cry out.

But Grams, she just says, "Cause you're wicked. Now let me finish the purge. Chango, mondongo, mofongo, bacalao. Chuleta, chancleta panti pa'fuera."

I didn't wanna disappoint her; I knew this could be her last exorcism. So I'd start speaking in tongues and turning into Satan. I'd start jumping around and shaking and muttering in Hebrew and Arabic, Italian and ancient Chinese. Then I'd say, "I am Satan the cloven-hoofed. I've come to claim you as my wife. Come here, crusty old lady."

"Here I am, Satan—take me," Grams offered.

And then I'd have to remind her, "But it's just me, Grams. Your little Johnny."

She'd snap right out of it and slap me. "Don't you ever summon Satan again, cabroncito malcriado.

"This is for Jesus *(slap!)* and this is for La Virgin Mary *(slap!)* and this is for making me miss happy hour!" *(slap! slap! slap!)*

"But Grama, it's only seven-thirty," I'd point out.

"Oh, good, I still have twenty minutes, then." And off she'd go.

THIRD-WORLD LOGIC

N ow our apartment was so puny it wished it were a project. It was a seventies nightmare; our walls were avocado green with brown linoleum and a nuclear orange shag rug; we were trying to re-create the papaya of our tropix and those seventies lamps that hung like an alien eyeball staring at us. And the centerpiece, the pièce de résistance of this mess, was our TV, my dad's pride and joy. It was sacred to him, because my pops could Latinize everybody in America; we would let the screen get real dusty so that everybody looked nice and dark and Spanish. And my father was the only one allowed to watch TV, cause he thought the more you watch it, the more you wear it out. Dad was operating under some kind of third-world logic.

He'd say, "Don't use my television and don't sit on my furniture unless we have important guests. Use the floor for sitting and the kitchen sink for eating. And we're not gonna buy any more food if you keep eating it! Food, I repeat, is for the guests and the animals. And I just brushed the dogs, so don't pet 'em! And get the hell off the rug, I just vacuumed it. And stop sucking up all my oxygen—I'm breathing it."

My brother and I would be like, "Okay, Dad, okay."

I was a prisoner in my own house. I felt like . . . Anne Frank. Except she only had Nazis to deal with. And every time my father had something important to say, the subway would go by. And it wouldn't have been a problem, but we shared a wall with the number 7 Train.

He'd start lecturing us, "I'm only gonna say this once. The most important thing I want you to do is . . ." and sure enough the train would roar by, drowning him out ". . . or I'm gonna kick your ass!"

Paralyzed with fear, I'd say, "Okay, Dad—no problem."

But as soon as my father was out of the house, my brother Poochie and I would be like a Navy SEAL operation. "Now, Poochie," I'd say, "it's 1800 hours, and the *Prince of Darkness* will be . . ."

Poochie freaked out. "Prince of Darkness? You didn't tell me nuttin' about no Prince of Darkness. Na-ah, I'm not listening. Mamaku mamasa mama mamakus . . ." He put his hands over his ears and closed his eyes.

"Poochie," I'd have to yell, "the Prince of Darkness is the man you know as Dad. Now you go put the bubble wrap under the rug so when Dad comes through the hall we'll hear him. Now we're punishment-proof. We outsmarteded that ignor-anus! What a maroon! What a sucker-butt! Ha ha! *Ungawa ungawa, Dad's away for two hours. A beep beep, we're TV freaks. Get stupid.* Poochie, turn the TV on." Then we'd settle down for a TV frenzy—"Spiderman," "Underdog," "Gigantor" the space robot. Everything was great until I messed with the antenna. I'd be swinging around in time to the "Spiderman" theme when suddenly . . . SNAP! The blood drained out of my body and into the ground and back to Latin America. "Poochie, I broke the antenna!"

And just then, "John!" Luckily, it was just my moms.

"Mom. Why are you climbing in through the window?" I wondered.

"The rent is due. What the hell are you doing? You're sitting on the furnitura. You're eating the food. Ay, dios mio, you broke the antenna!! Oh my God! I'm looking into the face of a dead boy." Moms had a knack for calming me down.

"Mom, use me for cruel animal experimentation, sell me to child pornographers, but don't let him get his hands on me!!!" I begged, throwing myself around her legs.

"No, don't, don't. I'll miss you. But now I must distance myself," she said. "Come, Poochie, you're an only child now. Ciao. Get off me, John. Get off."

Then all of a sudden we hear the sound of snapping bubble wrap and Pop's voice, cursing, "Cono, qué es toda esta mierda de bubble wrap, hijo de puta."

So I'm blowing and fanning the TV, cause my pops would feel it for heat. And my moms goes into rescue mode, "I'll take care of your father," she whispered to me as Pops came in. "Fausto, you look so ultra sexy. You look so sexy. Yes, you do. Let's have a game of one-on-one?" Moms flashed a breast at my father, pulling out all the stops. "You and me. One-on-one."

But my father wasn't taking the bait. "Woman, put that nipple away. I just wanna watch my television. C'mon fellas."

My moms tried another approach. "Good, good. Okay, then, why don't you go downstairs and play pool. Hmm? Okay? Play some pool?"

God bless my moms. We didn't have a downstairs.

Pops turned on the TV. "I said no, woman. What the hell's all that static. I can't tell Sonny from Cher."

"I'll fix it! I'll fix it!" I offered, right away. So I moved the good piece of antenna for all I was worth. "Like this, Dad? Or this? Here?"

"Move the other one!" Pops barked.

So I pretended to move the broken antenna. *Trompe l'oeil*. I frantically shifted my body around while holding the broken antenna in place. "There? Like so? Perfect?" I was using up all my available cuteness.

"Move away from that television," Pops ordered.

"Okay, I am away," I said, inching over a bit.

"Get the hell out of the room, you little shit!" Pops yelled. I stayed in the same place but moon-walked.

"Okay, I'm leaving the room, the neighborhood . . ." and as I head for the door, I trip. He sees the antenna came off in my hand. "It's a spear and I'm a hunter?" I offer meekly. I know what's coming next.

My pops field-goals me with a kick across the room. Luckily the nice hard brick wall broke my fall. And my head opened up like a piñata. "Dad, look at the pretty candy," I cooed. Then everything went black. And as I was waiting to die, my life started flashing before me. Yachting on the Cape, debutante orgies at Vassar, Monet sunsets on the Riviera. Wait a minute—that's not my life. And I felt my soul leave my body and hover over, and I looked down and— "damn, why didn't anybody tell me I had such a flat face," and I sailed out the window toward the light higher and higher, and I remembered my comix and how Spiderman once said to Ironman, "That to escape the pain, one must move toward the pain." And my soul thought, "Fuck that noise!" and sprinted the hell outta the house, and into the sky . . . and as I flew closer to the light, I saw a divine being, a beautiful woman standing there naked, her pert breasts glistening in the moon beams, and I wanted to suckle the breasts of all nurturing unconditional loves, and her arms were outstretched, beckoning me toward her . . . and just when I was about to touch her, I caught a whiff of my favorite Chino Latino restaurant, shrimp fried rice and platano maduro, and suddenly I wanted to live. If only for the plantanos, I wanted to live and *boom,* I was back in my body with all this new-found wisdom. The first words out of my mouth said it all:

"Poochie broke the antenna."

Poor, slow, chubby Poochie. I watched him go off screaming and yelling, "No! Don't! Anything but that. I'm your favorite. Remember, Dad?" And I just stood there watching, the only brother I had, beaten senseless with the antenna, and all I could think was, "Thank God it's not me." But I don't wanna leave you with a bad impression of my pops. Cause he wasn't always this brutal. No, sometimes he drank, too.

And when my pops drank he became the most loveable son of a bitch in the land. And he'd go out on the fire escape and he'd sit me on his knee and he'd start with the hugs and the playful teasing and he'd start wailing to old-world songs.

"Vivo solo sin tí/Sin poderte olvidar/Un momento no más/Vivo pobre de amor/A la espera de quién/No me dá una ilusión/Miro el tiempo pasar/Y al infierno llegar/Todos menos a tí/Si otro amor me viniera a llamar no lo quiero ni oir . . . oir . . ." He trailed off when he forgot the lyrics. "I proposed to your mother with this song; boy, was she easy. Having a good time? You enjoying this? Good, cause I'm gonna take it all away from you. Then you'll really know how miserable life can be. You know, it's time you start providing for this family."

"But I'm only ten, Pops."

"Oh, so now it's time to sit back and rest on your laurels, Mr. Big Shot? C'mere, I love you. What are you cringing at? Afraid of a little affection? I'm your father, you little faggot. Come on, give me a kiss. You kiss me or I'll punch the shit out of you."

"Okay, Dad." I went along with it and kissed him.

"Not on the lips, you little freak! You're so lucky to have a dad like me who comes home at all, when I would be out fucking hot, stinking women and having a great time, but am I doing that? No, because I'm right here spending quality time with my loser of a son." Then Pops would whistle for my mom. "Hey, woman, bring your big fat ass over here, I wanna look at it. Can you believe you were squeezed out of those two butt cheeks? Mmm. But it's home." Then he'd try to get me to drink a little. "Come on, you punk, have a shot. C'mon, it's just happy juice."

But I wouldn't touch the stuff. "Na-ah, it tastes like dookie. Dad, why don't you just quit drinkin'?"

"Cause I'm not a quitter. Drink it," he said, "and I'll give you ten bucks."

"Deal! But let me see the money first. Oh, okay. I trust you." I took a swallow. "Euw. That's good. Now where's my money?"

"Where's *my* money not to tell your mother you're a little alcoholic?" Pops asked.

I called out for Moms right away.

"Who do you think your mother's gonna believe—me or your Cuervo breath?" Pops pointed out.

He had a point. I gave in. "I'll have another round." My head started spinning. "I love you, Dad. I really do."

"That's my boy," he said, watching me take another pull on the bottle. "That's why I'm gonna tell you my secret scheme. And if you tell anybody, I'll have to kill you. Bobo pendejo, I'm gonna rent every room in this apartment till I own the building, the block. I'm gonna be King of Tenements, the Latino Donaldo Trumpo. I'm gonna elevate my situation, I'm gonna be an entrepreneurial business man, not a servant. Cause a servant serves and I don't want to serve."

"Cause my dad's no servant," I yelled, clinking glasses with him.

"All right, calm down. Someday you're gonna be the Crowned Prince of Tenements, Johnito."

"You're a regular genius, Dad. I'm so glad we could be this close. I always pictured it like this. You and me and the stink of alcohol. Dad, I got a secret too." I took another sip to steady myself. "It was me who broke the antenna. See, I knew you'd understand." I made a scramble for the window, but Pops grabbed my leg and pulled me back out to the fire escape.

"Dad! No, Dad! Mom! It was really Poochie, like I said the first time. No! Dad, don't!"

Those were some of the best times I had with my father, but of course with the onslaught of puberty, I quickly realized I could have a much better time alone.

19

THE FIRST ORGASM

I was about twelve the first time I tried to masturbate. I thought I broke it, cause something that wasn't pee actually leaked out and I was like, "Ahh!" I actually thought I spilled the glue that kept it together. But it felt so good that pretty soon I was becoming unglued every chance I got. About ten times a day and experimenting. I wanted to feel the whole world through my penis. "I wonder what it would feel like if I touch a sandwich with my penis? Ooh, mayonaisey. What if I touch it to glass? Ooh, cold! My dog?" (You're sick—I know what you're thinking.)

I could play with it all day long. "Arise, Sir Loin-of-beef," I said, tapping an imaginary subject with my newly found "sword." "Now let me see if I can lift this chair with the phone book, the radio, and the shoes on it. Okay, maybe just the chair. Okay, how about just a tie? Aha! Success! Damn, I'm a monster. Don't be frightened." I tied a Windsor knot in the tie. "Now I'm ready for company." Then I would begin the fun part. "Okay, let me see if I can hit that Kristy McNichol poster, bounce and strike my Six-Million-Dollar-Man action figure, then hit Grams' blood-pressure medicine, and ricochet into the toilet. My load d'amour finally landed. Oops, my brother's toothbrush. Oh well, he never uses it anyhow."

Out of nowhere, my pops is at the door. "Come on, you little punk. You're not doing what I think you're doing, are you? Not in my house, you don't!"

"No! Leave me alone! I'm going mad," I shouted through the door as I continued to ferociously masturbate.

But my kid brother, Poochie, whom I renamed "the boy called bitch," decides to be all helpful. "I'll let you in, Dad. I know how to open the door, Dad. Blame the antenna on me, will he?" I heard him mutter to himself.

The door kicks open and my whole family rushes into the bathroom, and there I am, totally naked, perched on the sink and my moms goes, "You are dead to me! I can't look." But then she peeks, appreciatively. "Ay, John!"

"What the hell are you doing in here?" my dad yells.

I think fast. "See, I was about to take a shower when I decided . . . I needed . . . to . . . change the lightbulb."

"With your erect penis?" he asks.

"Um . . . I couldn't reach with my hands?" I try, hopefully.

"And why are your moms' panties on your head?" he continues.

"I couldn't find my shower cap?" I try, again.

"What's this goo on my toothbrush, John?" Poochie asks.

"That's my . . . new toothpaste?"

Dad says, "Then prove it! Brush your teeth. Now."

"But . . . but . . . I don't wanna brush my teeth! Grama . . . please!" I start to beg.

"I'm not touching that cum," Grams states.

And that was the dental-hygiene crossroads for my family, cause no one really ever brushed with confidence again.

FELLAS ON SEX

So my father put a glass door on the bathroom, so I was forced to look elsewhere for my sexual exploration. And luckily about that time we started going to house parties. Where the homies would be on one side and the homettes on the other. And my crew of inner-city misfits would be huddled together sharing misinformation about the secrets of sex.

My friend Bobo said, "Yo, you have to pork a girl as fast as you can or it'll close up on you and lock up on your wood. And there's a bitch attached to you wherever you go and what not. I'm serious. No joke, kid."

Then Lollipop offered his wisdom. "Yo, a wet dream can be dangerous if you sleep with an electric blanket. Word 'em up."

My friend Xerox, he's dancing around, and he says, "Yo, pulling on your dick makes it biggerer. Not that I need to know this info—this is for ya'lls benefit. You know what I'm saying, John?"

So, I've got to hop in and show 'em I know what's what. "A menstrual cycle has . . . three wheels."

"Yeah, whatever, John," Bobo says. "Yo, let's have a 'who dick bigger' contest. My dick is five fingers plus a small X-men Wolverine action figure. Ha ha."

Xerox says, "Dag, mine's the size of a Devil Dog with the end bit off. Ha ha. You know what I'm sayin'."

So I say, "Mine's like a can of tuna," and they look at me weird till I continue, "cause you know it's the width that counts!"

FRESH-AIR FUNK

I was a very misunderstood child. So my parents finally got sick of my friends' influence on me and my strange sexual blatherings and signed me up with the Fresh-Air Fund for the summer. That's where they take a poor underprivileged disenfranchised kid and have him stay with a rich New England family. They expand your horizons, show you how great and fun life can be, and then just when you're getting comfortable—three meals a day, lead-free paint chips—they snatch it all away. So if you didn't know how poor you were, now your ass really knows!

There was one horrible thing that the Fresh-Air Fund faculty hadn't prepared me for: men born in this country don't have foreskins. I thought everybody was like me until I walked in on my Fresh-Air brother. It was in one of those outdoor showers that I saw my first circumcised penis.

"Oh, dag. What's wrong with you?" I asked. "You're a mutilated mutant, you silly little freak."

And then my other Fresh-Air brother walks in and he has the same deformity.

"What's wrong with you people?" I asked.

Then the father comes in and he's scarred, too.

"Oh, my God, it's a colony of mutants. It must be the water. You're mutants. Mutants. Weirdos."

But then my Fresh-Air Fund brother says, "Father, what's wrong with him? Look at all that skin."

And the other brother chimes in, "It looks like a slug."

"No, no," disagrees the first brother. "I think it looks like a mouse in a garden hose."

"Now, now. Don't make fun, boys," scolds the Fresh-Air Fund father. "Little John comes from a primitive land where they don't have the benefits of running water and surgery. If your grades aren't good and you're disobedient and you don't get into the Ivy League, your foreskins will grow back and eventually cover your face, skin, and body, and possibly even your loved ones."

But all I can say is, "You don't like it? It's my anteater. It's a protective covering not unlike a turtleneck."

I thought it was a conspiracy. Why didn't anybody tell me? For years after that I showered in my jeans—cause you never know. But back in the city I wasn't afraid to show my penis, cause everybody's was like mine, just bigger.

Every evening in my Fresh-Air Fund household, we'd gather around a roaring fire. I don't know why. It was summertime . . . And my Fresh-Air Fund father would hold forth. "You see, little brown man, people of good breeding sip cognacs and talk about lacrosse, and pet their golden retrievers." He took a big puff on his pipe. "I think I'll forego all social activities tonight. Goodnight, little inner-city foundling. Let's go upstairs, honey-bunny; I feel f-r-i-s-k-y."

Like I don't know how to spell *fry-sky*. I knew they were about to sex up. And I ran and hid under their bed, hoping for some wild adult porn. But all I heard were these real quiet squeaks.

Then my Fresh-Air Fund father says, "Oh, oh, thank you, dear." And my Fresh-Air Fund mother says, "No, let's not make it worse by talking. Goodnight."

Now it was a whole 'nother ball game at my aunt Anissette's up in Spanish Harlem with her and her lover/mechanic guy, and they'd be, like . . . "Take this and that and some of this. Take it all, you whore, you slut, you bitch."

And then he would say, "I know I can't never truly satisfy you, but at least I fuck you, right?"

And my aunt Anissette would yell, "Wrong! No, you don't fuck me, I fucks you. A'right? And you call that fucking? I didn't even know you was in the room. Ay, please!"

JEWISH RESORT

By the end of that summer, my pops' tenement scheme had finally paid off. And when I got back from the Fresh-Air Fund I hardly recognized him. He became Nuyorican rich, which meant he started wearing fake fur coats and fake gold chains. He was a cross between Huggy Bear and Mr. Roper. Since Dad had now "made it," he wanted to join a fancy country club, but the WASPs said, "No fucking way." So we went to the second-best thing: a Jewish country club, and we got in because of a little white lie.

Our waiter would greet us, "Ah, are you the rich Leguizam-bergs of Jackson Heights? Well, your table is right here. Beware the pogroms. It'll start all over again, but you with such a lovely family. And, kine-ahora, who are these lovely children? You little bubbala. You must be kvelling. Their names?"

My pops, in his fur coat and chains, thought fast. "This is . . . Abraham. This is Moses. Say thank you, Abraham!"

"Thank you," I said. But Pops said, "Smile." I smiled. "More Jewish," he said. I smiled wider.

And a few weeks into the summer, disaster struck—over the P.A. system, loud as can be, came an announcement: "Would Mr. Leguizam-berg go to the front desk, immediately."

And my dad marched—all self-righteous—fronting like he'd won a mahjong set, with his fake fur coat flowing behind him.

The manager was buffing his nails, waiting. "Mr. Leguizam-berg. We have a very nice resort that caters to a certain . . . classy clientele and they expect a certain courtesy . . ."

"And your point is?" my dad interrupted.

"Your children are—how can I put this delicately?—foul-mouthed primitives . . . and they shit in the pool."

"And?" Pops prompted.

"Well, then they started to throw it at each other."

"So?" Pops was patiently waiting for the point.

"They were throwing their own shit!" The manager yelled.

My pops just shrugged. "It's what kids do. You throw some to a friend, and he throws it back to you. Throwing shit is part of a happy childhood."

Then all of a sudden my cousin Speedy appeared in the doorway. "Your house got on fire and completely burned down. Grama Dulce fell asleep with a cigar in her mouth," Speedy gasped.

My pops was silent, stunned. Then he got all choked up. "Look at my kids down there. So innocent and young . . . throwing their own shit. Not knowing what they lost. Why me, God? Why me? Always out to get the littlest guy, always fucking over the humble. Here, you wanna fuck somebody? You wanna do somebody up the anus, God? Here, take Speedy."

Now, I don't know if it was the loss of his tenement, the loss of his standing in the Jewish community, or the way he talked to God, but he couldn't take it no more, and was arrested in a nearby mall, naked, stealing pennies out of the fountain and claiming he was invisible. And my moms was all upset. "Children, don't look. Officer, is there anything you can do?"

But Pops barged right in. "Do? There's nothing he can do. Because I'm invisible. What's causing that mysterious splashing? What strange power is causing your pants to fall down unexpectedly, breaking all the laws of space and time? 'Tis I—the *invisible* Tenement King."

After my dad undid that cop's pants—he became the *unconscious* invisible Tenement King.

SURROGATE MOMS

With Dad unavailable, my moms had to take up the slack. And times were tight—every day of every month we ate Shake 'n Bake. Right out of the box. We couldn't afford the chicken. When they came out with Shake 'n Bake Barbecue, it was a fucking national holiday in my house. And since my moms was working so much, my uncle Sanny became our surrogate moms. Now, my uncle Sanny was a little unconventional. He was what you'd call a triple threat: Latin, gay, and deaf. And he was so wise he was dubbed the Einstein of Jackson Heights.

"Ay, fo," Sanny exclaimed. "I know things even God doesn't know! Ay, puta, que escándalo, me jodí. At Christmas I always made a lousy Santa. Instead of filling the stockings, I was always trying them on, Ay, fo! Poof, bad thoughts be gone. Ay, que escándalo, me jodí, la loca dame huevo."

I loved him and I told him so. "I wanna grow up and be just like you, uncle Sanny, except for the liking men part."

"I know your father doesn't respect me," Sanny said, "but that's bullshit. Because feature this: many highly respectable individuals of ancient and modern times have been homosexuals: Plato, Michelangelo, Disney. Oops, I outed him. Que escándalo, lo jodí."

Just cause we were poor didn't mean we didn't get culture. Cause one day my uncle Sanny took us to Broadway, The Great White Way. He finessed this technique he coined "Second acting." First we mixed in with the intermission smokers and then we tried to slip into the theater undetected to catch the second act.

"John, Poochie, here, smoke these," Uncle Sanny said. "Uh-uh-uh, Menthol for you, Poochie. You're only twelve. No, they're not children, they're midgets."

So with stolen programs in hand we waited for everyone to sit down, then we ran down the aisles and grabbed the empty seats.

I wasn't sitting with anyone I knew and I'm scared of being clocked and I'm peeping at this ridiculous musical *Chorus Line* thing when I hear somebody called Morales on stage. There was a Latin person in the show. And she didn't have a gun or hypodermic needle in her hand and she wasn't a hooker or a maid and she wasn't servicing anybody so it was hard to tell if she was Latin and everybody's respecting her and admiring her . . . I was lost in this amazing moment, singing along as loud as I could. Then I felt a hand grab me and I was yanked up out of my seat by one of those Pilgrim ladies and beat with the flashlight. My brother got caught, too, cause he was still smoking his Kools, and Sanny got busted, cause he was lip-syncing along too loudly. And I'm still like, "She's singing to me, she's singing to me!" And Uncle Sanny's yelling, "Shut the hell up and run! Run!" And that's how I got culture.

FRENCH PASSING—NOT!

Meanwhile my pops was scheming it. To keep food on the table he finally hit with the luck of the Latin and got a job as the headwaiter at the top French restaurant in Manny Hanny. And my brother Poochie's birthday came around and I thought I would give him an extra nice surprise and take him to Dad's restaurant. So we put on our best leisure suits and subwayed it into Manhattan.

"John, we're not supposed to be in here. Dad's gonna open up a can of kick ass on us," Poochie worried.

"This is a birthday surprise for you and Dad, fat boy."

"I don't want to be called fat boy no more, John, I'm a man now."

"Okay, fat man," I conceded.

The waiter talked like he smelled something bad. "Bonjour. What will you be having, young sirs?"

"No offense, Mr. Garçon, sir, but we'd like to be served by the *head*waiter, Mr. Leguizamo," I insisted.

"I'm not sure I'm familiar with that name," our waiter drawled.

"You must be new here, cause our dad runs this place. Why don't you make yourself useful and go find him, mister man, sir." I rolled my eyes at Poochie. "The help."

And I'm looking around for Dad and looking and I can't see him anywhere and he doesn't show up and there's only so much olive oil we could drink. And the kitchen doors swing open long enough so I can see a guy that looks a lot like my dad, but I know it can't be him, cause that guy's bending over a sink washing dishes. But then they swing open again. I look real closely. We had to get outta there.

I yank Poochie's leg. "Come on, Poochie. All of a sudden I'm not in the mood for French. The sauces are too rich. I'm afraid I'll get male breasts. Let's get a pizza."

But Poochie pouts. "I'm not leaving till I see Dad order somebody around, John."

"You see that at home all the time. Every day. Now come on, Poochie, let's go, little man." I pull him toward the door.

"John, you ruined my birthday. I'll take pizza, but it better be large and no anchovies on my pizza. You think one of my legs is longerer than the other? John, why aren't you talking to me?" I was quiet as Poochie rambled on.

S
o I was an angry, disillusioned kid. And then we up-
graded to a poor all-Irish neighborhood in Sunnyside,
Queens, where we were the first Latin family, so we were
like pioneers. Manifest destiny in reverse. And I see this
real hot Irish chick. You know the type—red-headed, freckled, drunk,
lapsed Catholic whore, ready to be inseminated by a wily Latin stud.
Okay, I'm bitter—they never liked me. So I'm having some green
beer, and since everybody's Irish on St. Patrick's Day I figured I'll try
out my gift and riverdance over to her, and I talk to her in the thickest
Irish accent I can manage.

"Toy, hello, lassie, how's the Emerald Isle? You ever fuck a lep-
rechaun? Erin go bragh and begorrah. Why are you looking at me
like that? Is my shillelagh hanging out? Are my shenanigans banging about out?"

She took a long draw on her cigarette and said, "You don't look
Irish to me."

"Oh, but I am, black Irish." I lifted my beer. "I'm parched above, lassie. Are you moist below?"

Okay, so I didn't say that. I said how much I respect Irish culture and what contributions they've made: U2, whiskey, cops, and, of course, Scotty. "Captain, the dilithium crystals are breaking up, the engine she's gonna blow. The heath the moor you know you got to go see *Trainspotting, Braveheart.* You sit through the whole movie and you can't understand a word even if you see it forty times."

"What kind of fucking moron are you?" she asked.

"Scotty's Scottish, asshole. Everybody knows that. Brian, Sean, Blarney, this Spanish guy is bothering me."

Then ten or fifteen of her hooligan brothers circled me, proof that the rhythm method doesn't work in the Irish community. We Latin people, we have rhythm, but we save it for dancing.

"Are you trying to get with our sister, you dirty Puerto Rican?" asked the biggest Irish brother.

"Well, your mother was booked, now wasn't she?" I remarked.

"I'll wipe up the street with ya, you little wetback!" He took a threatening step in my direction.

"But where, laddie? Where's the lad with the moist back?" I cried out, looking all around the bar. "I'll give him a taste of me fisticuffs. Where's the little fucker? I'll find the little fucker and get him for you."

"You! You're the lying little spic!" He wasn't fooled.

I was outnumbered, but I didn't care. I did what any proud Latin kid raised in the ghetto would do in that situation, and I make no apologies. I—acted like a retard. "I didn't touch the pretty lady, no I didn't. I gotta pee. Hold it for me. Why won't you hold it for me? It burns. Come on, blow on it. Why won't you blow on it?"

S o we had to move, to Corona, which was an all-Italian neighborhood, so I was excited to be welcomed by our fellow swarthy, olive-skinned Mediterranean brothers and sisters. "Mira, oye, grazie prego, Pacino, De Niro."

My new Italian friend responded warmly. "You spic. You dumb fucking ugly dumb dumb fucking ugly dumb dumb ugly fucking dumb dumb dumb . . . Hey, Joey, did I use up dumb already?"

"Yeah, Ant-knee. Try . . . douchebag?"

"Yeah, you douchebag douchebag fucking bobouchebag banan-afana fo fucking fouchebag fe fi fo mo mouchebag fucking douche-bag forget about it. Youse douchebags ruined this neighborhood. Before youse came here there were nice houses and great stores, no doubt about it."

"Yeah, yeah, I know; we Latin people are the bacteria of the uni-verse," I admitted. "We're lazy, we fuck too much, and look what I bought with my welfare check—a Guido joke book! And to think I almost wasted it on crack. Here's one I'm sure you'll like. How can you tell if your baby's a Guido? Give up? He won't use a pacifier un-less it's got hair on it. That means that your mother has hair on her nipples. I like that one. That shit can't be true. You're the Guido, you tell me. Oh, shit, ha, ha, ha. Why aren't you laughing?"

They started stomping me and yoking me. So I did what any Latin kid would do in that situation—I acted like a retard again. "I gotta pee. Will you hold it for me?"

Unfortunately, they knew my Irish friends. "Hey, this is the clown the Irish Mic warned us about. You fucking bozo, I got a retarded brother. Give me my homey-be-good stick."

He started swinging at me so I tried another strategy. "Ow, ow. Yo, wait up . . . wait up fellas. I have . . . Tourette's. I have no control over what I say—it's completely involuntary, it just comes out, you fucking moron piece of white trash suck my long brown dick and like it like your mother does," I barked, and twitched and jerked around for effect. "I'm sorry. I'm really sorry. I don't know what came over me, saying that about your mother liking my dick and all, it's the Tourette's."

They bought it. "Oh, wow, it's horrible. Is there a cure for torres?"

"No, it's terminal and extremely contagious." Then I breathed on them. "Can I hang out with you guys?"

They ran off.

FIRST LOVE—

BLACK VENUS

So we had to move again. Now as much as the Irish and the Italians hated me, I finally found a girl who loved me, and my grandfather said to me, "John, you have three loves in your life. Don't waste them. Now pull the plug." I knew she was going to be the first one. She was my ebony princess, my Nubian bucket of love, my Africanus romanticus. She was black and her pops was a Black Muslim, so when it finally came time to meet him, I thought, "This guy might be my future father-in-law." I came over in my best Elijah Muhammad bow tie and said, as nerdily as I could, "Hello sir, I'm here to pick your daughter up for a date."

Her black pops met me at the door, sucking on his teeth and popping out his cheek. "You don't fool me, boy. You don't look like a Muslim with that bow tie—you look like Pee-Wee Herman, and when I look at your white skin I wanna kill you."

"But I'm not white sir, I'm a Latino."

"Well, then I definitely don't wanna get caught up in an illegal-alien Mexican situation. I heard about you Mexicans, buying up all the Cabbage Patch dolls just to get the birth certificates," he said.

So I would have to sneak up to her window at night to avoid her pops, and I'd stand there and profess my undying love. "I love you, Yashica."

"What did you say?!" she yelled.

She lived on the fifty-eighth floor.

"I'll love you forever!!" I screamed again.

Then the neighbors called out, "Yeah, we love you, too—now shut the fuck up and go to sleep." So she met me at the service elevator, then snuck me into her room. And it was so romantic—we put on some Al Green, she turned on the black light, we took off article after article of clothing till we were in our underwear only and I was about to finally lose my virginity. I looked at my beautiful black Venus. She looked at me.

Then she said, "Oh, my God, you are the whitest motherfucker I ever saw. You glow in the dark."

"I love you, Yashica," I responded.

"Yeah, whatever. You don't get it, Translucent Man. Oh, my God— turn around for a second. I can see your intestines, like a guppy. I can tell what you had for lunch. Hold on, hold on, I want my sister to see your blue veiny ass, guppy boy. Shanté. Shanté, come here, girl."

KENTUCKY FRIED

DE-VIRGINIZING

So I was still a virgin. So for my sixteenth birthday, Dad, seeing his son's miserably failed attempts at becoming a man, decided to give nature a little push.

He got the car out and loaded us in. "Hey, John, Poochie, get in back." My dad suddenly got serious. "John, you know since the average pinga is six inches and the average vaginga is eight inches, there are two miles of unused vaginga in New York City and I'm gonna find some for you. Okay, here we are. Poochie, wait in the car."

"Kentucky Fried Chicken. How's the Colonel gonna make me a man?" I wondered.

"Not the Colonel, stupid. It's a lady who works here. She fries/batters chickens by day and chokes chickens by night."

And the next thing I know I'm in the back of the Kentucky Fried Chicken and this mad, fine, stout German lady in her late forties comes out. "Your swarthy looks are so dark and I feel sorry for you, so I will fuck you. I'll think of it as war reparations."

So she has me over the fryer and we're sucking face. Then she reaches down and touches my Thing. It was the first time someone other than me had touched it, so as you can imagine, my Thing's buggin' out.

I can hear it talking to me. "Uh, Johnny, what's she doing?"

"Just relax. We're getting some," I try to reassure my Thing.

"Um, she's being a little rough—she's pulling, Johnny!"

"She's German. Now will you shut up?!!"

My Thing is not giving up. "Johnny, can't you just do it? I like how you do it. You know where to touch, what I like . . . What I need . . ."

Then she put the whole thing in her mouth.

Suddenly, my Thing is singing a different tune. "Ooh! Why didn't you ever do this?"

I told him, "I couldn't reach!"

Now, you know how people always say that time distorts memory. Details change. Exaggeration occurs with the retelling. But not in this case. Before I could think, she'd stripped down and put my hand on her little vertical smile. Her coochie was a failed experiment from *The Island of Dr. Moreau*. Now, I'm man enough to admit that I've been confused about female genitalia. You never know what you're gonna get. You're always in dark light. And you always have to pretend to know what you're doing, so you never really get a good look. If I saw one coming at me in the light of day I'd probably take a snow shovel to it. Then she does the international cunnilingus sign and coaches me.

"It's like a flower. You have to unravel it."

So with the courage of Jacques Costeau on his last expedition, I started to unravel and unravel and unravel her huge coochie lips. It was like Dumbo. If she could flap them she would be able to fly out of the room and back to Germany. When I opened it all, it made a Tupperware burp.

And then my Thing, the little general, gets scared and starts talking to me again. "No. Hell no. I'm not going in there. I like the mouth."

But I didn't want to disappoint my pops, so I had to sacrifice the little general. In he went. I was like a porn star: "You like that street dick. That nasty Latin seed." So I started working her right in the fried chicken batter, this way and that way, up and down. And she's like, "No, over *here*, honey." "Oh, I'm sorry. It's my first time," I explained. Breast and thighs are flying up in the air—not hers, the chickens'. We're in a cloud of flour. And finally in her moment of orgasm, a stream flew out of her. I was soaking. Marinated in her juices.

"Hey, did you just . . . No, you didn't just . . . did you? I can't believe what I'm gonna say. Did you just pee on me?" I asked.

"No, it's the way I cum. It's another gift. See, my urethra is connected to my clitoris, and when my pubogeneous muscles contract . . ."

"You share too much, lady," I interrupted. "I just want to cuddle."

But my time was up, so she went over to the window, grabbed a coochie lip in each hand, and jumped. She flew away into the night like a giant pink bat. Bye, Mothra.

When I came out to the car, Pops was all questions. "How did you do? Give her the eighth ingredient, hijo?"

"Yeah, I did it!"

"But how do I know? I need proof," Pops persisted.

"Proof? Proof?" I wrang my shirt out and wiggled my toes, which made a squishy sound. "There's your proof."

"That's my boy!" Pops beamed. "Now we've shared this!"

DOMESTIC VIOLINS

I had become a man, and back home my moms was becoming her own woman—getting radical, going to college and using big words against my pops—acting like she was going places like some disco queen. Meanwhile, my pops wouldn't let his tenement dream die, so our house looked like a construction site, and he had to keep working at the French restaurant. It made my pops all stressed out, so he became the Grinch who stole Christmas. "There will be no laughter nor happiness again or singing in this house." And my moms got home one day and she's unnaturally happy.

She was humming, "Ah, freak out. Le chic. C'est freak."

Then the Grinch came back in. "Who said you could sing that thing? I am the king and *nothing* is what I say you should sing-sing sing! And you're late. That I really do hate. To be made to wait I don't appreciate. I just hate hate hate."

My moms looked tipsy and she took a big drag on her cigarette. "Ay, Fausto, you're being tan Dr. Seussian. Lateness is such an amorphous and bourgeois concept. But if you must know, Snoopy, it was cause I was swamped and backlogged with work and things," she said, taking off her high heels, "a ton of various sundry miscella-neousnessness,"

"And the day before you got here at midnight—what the hell was that about?" Pops demanded.

"See how hard I work for you?" said Moms, removing her fake eyelashes. "I'm practically a slave. Lincoln, emancipate me. Break my shackles."

"Every time you're late I either think you're having an affair or you're dead. And when I call the Emergency Room in a panic and you're not dead, I get really pissed off. I need my woman home taking care of my childrens. Have you looked at them lately? John's sickly-looking and stupid, and Poochie's fat and ugly," said Pops.

"Look, Poochie would still be fat and ugly no matter what time I got home, so don't talk down to me. Cause I'm not just about re-production anymore. I'm about me-production," Moms said as she brushed her hair. Meanwhile, back in the kitchen, I'm like . . .

"Poochie, Dad called you fat and ugly and Mom agreed."

"Close that goddamn kitchen door!" Dad screamed. "Do you wanna be known as belt face for the rest of your life? Woman, don't make me have to teach you what respect is."

"Ay, fo, like a dishwasher could teach me anything," Moms spat back.

"Be quiet. Sssh! Do you wanna traumatize the childrens?"

Now Moms couldn't be stopped. "Okay, no more talking! Quick, who am I?" and she mimed washing a dish.

My father dove at her and started choking her. She slapped him with one hand and choked him back with the other. And they start wrestling on the floor. It was just like watching the World Wrestling Federation on TV. "Sábado, sábado en Madison Square Garden. Lucha libre de la época. La gran pelea Leguizamo contra Leguizamo traído por Burger King el rey de las hamburguesas, y Baskin Robbins treinta y un sabores." It started to look like Moms was losing.

"I'm going to have to kill you," Pops yelled.

And Moms screamed, "You don't have to do anything you don't want. You're in America now."

I took my brother into the kitchen and said, "Yo, Poochie—Moms ain't doing so well. We got to double team him. You go in there and kick the shit out of him. And I'm a live on to tell the brave tale of how 'weak little fat boy' stood up to a ferocious maniac killer."

And Poochie stuttered, "B . . . b . . . b . . . But I can't."

"Poochie, this is no time to pretend to act like a retard," I said.

Then I see a shining big butcher steak knife that my dad used on his father once before, so it's like a family heirloom. So I run out there like a little Jean Claude Goddamn.

I give Pops my best kung fu crouch and hold up the knife. "If you touch my moms or anyone in this house ever again, you're a goner."

"John, get outta here. You don't understand. This is none of your business," Pops yelled.

The butcher knife made me brave. "It is my business, so just get the fuck outta here! We're sick of you, Dad. Why don't you just get out and leave us all the fuck alone! Stop fucking up our lives and then taking it out on us. It's not our fault. Get out before we kill each other."

"You talk to your father like that," he seethed. "You're threatening me? You think you're man enough to take me, boy?"

"No, but I'm a do my best," I promised.

"Put that knife down," he demanded.

"No."

"Put it down."

Pops lunged at me and we struggled. I held onto that knife with both hands, but he got it away. "I hate you," I cried out, falling to my knees.

My father looked down at me. "I'm sorry, mijo, I didn't mean to hurt you. I'm not a cruel person." He started putting on his hat and coat. "I hope your son never looks at you how you're looking at me. I'll leave. You know, John—I came here to work. I didn't come here to crawl, but I didn't care, cause all I ever wanted was milk for my kids and beer for me, and always remember in life there are no do-overs or repeats, so if you don't do what you want—you'll end up like me."

THIS was the Dad that I had been wanting all my life. And there he was standing there all exposed. And finally, for a brief second, I saw him for who he really was: a hurt child. And I knew he was gonna tell me the words I'd been waiting for my entire life, and he turns to me and says . . . "Your mom's a puta bitch!"

Moms staggered back in shock.

"I'm not a puta bitch, John," my moms protested.

"So, then where'd she get that fancy mink coat when you and Poochie look like boat people? Dressed in Saran Wrap. And why does she wear that cheap perfume and sequin tube tops and see-through hot pants?" he persisted.

"Ay, Fausto, please. I may be paradoxical and mercurial, but I'm a damn good time. And what do you do that's so epiphenal?"

"I'm the King of Tenements, as soon as I finish some of this construction around here . . ." he trailed off.

"King of Tenements? You're the King of Holes, the Prince of Plaster. All I see around here is holes and plaster rock," Moms said contemptuously.

"That's it, Jezebel—get away from my childrens, you Salome, Samsonite and Delilah, get out of my house. You're a lousy wife, lousy cook, and all the big words in the world couldn't make you a good mother," Pops screamed. But he'd gone too far.

"Ex-cuseme, Ex-cuseme. Ex-cusme, 'Lousy mother' what? I gotta interfere on my own behalf, cause you can only fill a bottle so much before it spills over—and the lid just blew off this bottle!" My moms pushed me aside. "Move over, John. Fausto, ever since we've been together you've had the Midas touch in reverse—everything you touch turns to caca. I don't want your hand-me-down love, your sec-ondhand affection, your leftover sex . . . You don't get me twice in a lifetime. I want to quench the fire in my soul. I'm not a mat to be stomped, a rag to be rung, oh God, I'm not happy nor sad. I . . . I . . . I can't breathe."

"Easy, woman—you're having a breakdown," my pops inter-rupted.

"No, Fausto, I'm having a breakthrough. Don't touch me. Don't confuse the end of your world with the beginning of mine. I have awakened. Not now, John—I'm freaking out. I only have one more thing to say to you. Where did I put that eight-track tape? Thank you, John. I dedicate this to all my sister girlfriends who have been com-promised before me but gotten over in the end." And then she started singing the disco hit "I Will Survive." In the end, she flipped Pops the bird. "I'm gonna make up my own words, Fausto. I should've said this a long time ago. And listen good. You can't walk over me any-more. You want this fat ass, well, you can't have it anymore—aha. You made me into a bitch, Fausto, and I'm going to unbitch myself. No, Fausto, I can't be like other women. You know why, you wanna know why . . . ?" Just as the song was climaxing, Moms fell into a con-struction hole. "You and your holes, Fausto," she said, climbing out. Then she chimed in, again on the last few notes. "Hey, hey, Oh oh!" and she bowed and walked out.

That was a beautiful song and a nice moment for my moms, but unfortunately the house was under my father's name.

So my parents divorced and my father kicked us out of the house. And I went on my own to find myself. And I found out that I had a hard time being myself. I would rather be anybody than be myself—so I went to college. I had gotten a perfect 1600 on my SATs, if you count all four times I took it, so I went to that hot bed of academia, the Learning Annex, to get an associate's degree in the Decline of West Coast Civilization. And I was worried that I wasn't gonna fit in so I cleverly passed as a whiteboy, stayed out of the sun, straightened my hair, told people I was from California . . .

My surfer-boy act was not too convincing. "Malibu, to be exact. Oh, the rad waves, the whales, man, playing with dolphins, man, I communed with one. The things he shared with me. He explained the crimes of humanity in the name of tuna to me and I apologized."

So I got into a fraternity and at my initiation they kept trying to make me do shots and chug beer, but I was afraid if I did I would slip into urban, innercity minority lingo. So I was like . . . "No thanks, dude, trying to cut back. Taper off. No, I got nothing to hide."

But then one of my fraternity brothers comes over with these mushrooms. I had no idea what they were. "Oh, cool, crudité. I love vegetables." All of a sudden, things slowed way down. "What the fuck is happening to me? Nighty night, rabbit." I collapsed on the floor laughing. Then I took a good look at my new frat brothers and I started laughing harder. "Yo, you are the whitest mothafuckers I ever saw. Please, tell me your shit is white. Cono. Puñeta. Shit something out of your pretty white ass!"

The room goes silent. They sense an ethnic in their midst. "I'm having a bad trip. Later, dudes, I got crazy munchies," I say, trying to pull it back together.

So I go pig out at the cafeteria, ready to feast, when out of my peripheral vision I saw a Latino brother from the West Coast. He had an aura you could hear.

"Órale vato, La Raza, Latina paz simone," he greeted me.

"Yo, waz up my Hispanic brother?" I said, shaking his hand.

"Shut up, stupidl Stop talking shit! It's Latino, you colonized eunuch. Hispanic is the slave name given to us by the Spaniards in Iberia, and Iberia is Phoenician for land of the rabbits. And do I look like a rabbit to you, motherfucker? Do you think you look like a furry rabbit, ese?" he hissed.

"I like carrots," I said.

He was my first militant orthodox feminist vegan radical Latino separatist.

"Shut up! Why are you eating the food of the oppressor, ese?" he yelled.

"Chocolate pudding? Bill Cosby's black and he eats chocolate pudding," I defended myself.

"Shut up, stupid! Chocolate is oppressive, for it was pilfe . . . pilfereded . . . stolen from the temples of the Aztecs at the expense of thousands of warrior lives, homes. And it's an abomination, for it was forced to co-mingle with the Euro-fascist milk ripped from the bosom of innocent cows, which had been recently and peculiarly violated, simone," my Chicano brother ranted.

"Look, you gotta learn to talk regular to get by," I tried to point out, helpfully.

"I do talk regular," he said.

Just then my new trustafarian buds sauntered up. "Hey, *Jonathan*, is this suspicious character your bud?" one of them asked.

So I look them right in the eyes and muster up all my strength of will and character and say, "No. Oh, Jesus . . . I'm just directing him to his Affirmative Action booth. No poder hablar el español. No. No. Pero mucha graci-ass and de nalga," I say in my worst Spanish.

As we walked away, I saw a tear coming down the Chicano's face like that Indian in the sad garbage commercials. Anyway, I got kicked out of the fraternity cause my Chicano bro' outted me.

After that, I figured my acting must need work and I started to take it a little more seriously. So there I was, trying to get into Juilliard, one of the top acting schools, and I was there cause all the fine girls were there, too. So I do a Shakespeare monologue for my audition, which I fashioned from listening to Sir John Gielgud records. "Is this a dagger which I see before me the handle towards my hand come let me clutch thee."

But when I do it, it comes out like the ghetto classix. "Is this a dagger which I see before me? Yo, waz up with dat?"

Now I was on a roll. "What, ho! Ho. No, thou didn'tst. Thou besta talketh to thee back of thee hand, cause the fronteth ain't hearingth it, sirrah, out damned spot. My kingdom for a horse, or I wilst pimp slapeth thee and bitch slapeth thee. Oh, Juliet, alas alack, and a lick."

So I was rejected. The more rejection I got, the stronger I became—like some science fiction creature feeding on it.

I looked in the yellow pages and found Lee Strasberg was auditioning for his class, and there I am and all these actors are doing *Streetcar*, and all the women want to be Blanche DuBois and all the fellas want to be Brando. "Stella! Stella! What kind of queen do you think you are, sitting on that throne and swilling down my liquor. I say ha! Ha!"

After watching fifty Brandos, I knew I wouldn't pass, cause of my looks, so I didn't care. So I did my own take on it, Jerry Lewis style. And the acting teacher's like . . . "I survived the Holocaust, but I don't know if I can survive your performance. It's not very real. Dig deeper. Go to someplace painful in your past."

I immediately start wailing, "Poochie broke the antenna. It was Poochie."

I didn't get in there either, but I had found my gift: denial.

They may not have wanted me, but there was this Latina honey auditioning there—she remembered me and called me up. Her name was Boo Sanchez. She had a thick, home-girl accent. "I was nameded during Halloween, boo. Hilarious, right? Enough of me. My bad. And dog I was bugging when you went off, I mean . . . I loveded your Shakespeare—it was mad classical, right? Ai, please, I don't know what that jury's beef wichoo was, right? They are so mad corny? It was bomb. Pentameter. Iambic and all."

She got rejected, too. But we had each other. And I remembered what my grandfather said to me. He said to me, "John, you only get three loves in your life; don't waste them. Pull the plug." I used one up and the other one of mine had flown away. I wasn't gonna waste this one. Only thing is the mating ritual of the Latin woman is a little Jekyll and Hyde. We'd be sexing up and she'd be like, all of a sudden, "Animal, criminal, bestia, desgraciado, say you love me! Animal, criminal, zángano, sinberguenza, creído, arrogante, say you love me. Then lie. Lie the way you lied to get me here. I'm not in the mood anymore." Then she'd just stop and get water and pills.

"But baby, you said I was the best," I'd whine.

"No, no, I said you *did* your best. And besides, I have my gynecologist appointment tomorrow, and he told me not to have intercourse twenty-four hours ahead of time."

I saw a way around this. "Yeah, but you don't have a dentist appointment, do you?"

She was so self-sufficient and, honest, I fell madly, truly, and deeply in love. It was great to be with a real Latina who understood and completed me. Of course, my fear of intimacy drove my love away.

We'd be in the bathroom, getting ready for bed, and she'd start in. "Why you never say you love me? I mean, I don't wanna make you say it ..."

"Thank you, baby, cause I just feel . . ." And before I could even finish she'd say, "But I really think it would be in your best interest if you did. I just want it to come from you. I'm fine. It's not like I need it to get by. It's not like I'm living in an emotional vacuum. A black hole. I'm cool. I'm straight. I'm . . . Why you so afraid to say it?"

"I'm not afraid of saying it. I just think I've proven myself through action. I mean, what could words possibly add? And I experience my emotions on a preverbal level. To refine them through language is to change and pollute them. Now you don't want me to say 'I love you' and stop our relationship dead in its tracks, do you?"

I thought I had her here.

"Yes. Kill it. I wanna hear those words. Even if I never see you again. I wanna hear those words!!!"

"You want me to say 'I love you'? There. Is that better?"

"What did your parents do to you? This is your father's fault. I'm calling him." She went for the phone, but I stopped her. "Then you call him and make him give you a sign that he loves you—or you're never gonna be a man. All your life you're gonna feel guilty and alone unless he releases you. It's awful not to be loved. It's the worst thing in the world. I oughta know. You never say you love me to me. I hate you. Why are you so withholding? You really hurt me, John." She started sobbing. "I hate you. I hate my life. I wish I were dead." Then she'd scream at such a high pitch it was silent. When Latin women get upset, only dogs can hear them. So I'd ask my dog, "What she say, boy?"

Astro would let me know. "That bitch has had enough of your shit."

"Thanx, boy." So I leave her alone hoping she'll calm down and go into the living room for some food and I'm watching TV and she walks in and yells, "Who the hell told you you could watch my television!? And get off that couch. You know it's only for the guests!!"

I don't know how she got by the bubble wrap, but she did. And then the warm urine of realization flowed down my leg—holy shit, she's just like my pops. Well, I already had a father; I certainly didn't need that nonsense in a girlfriend. So I ended that mierda right there.

"Will you marry me?" I asked.

I know. I know. See, they tell you your whole life that you always marry your moms. Well, not me—I was gonna marry my pops.

So now my personal life was spoken for and I was looking for direction in my life, and I read in the paper that there was an open call and I met with this casting agent. I put on my lucky interview suit and went for it. "So what's the word?" I asked him.

"You're too ethnic. That's the word. What am I supposed to do with you? Start a reservation? They don't want a Hispanic—they want someone who can *play* a Hispanic. Wait—how do you feel about playing junkies?"

And I said, "Search no more, feast your eyes . . . Stop the world, I'm down."

So, *bam*, I'm in my first play. I show up at the theater for the first rehearsal all cocky, and the director's going . . . "More Latino. I wanna feel the agony and patheticness of your people."

So I'm really trying, giving it all I got. "I need a fix, man—come on, take my kid, anything."

"More pathetic, more Latino. More junkie, think Latino!" the director yells.

"I'm outta veins, I'll stick it in my neck, how about my eyeball? La metadona esta cabrona." I'm eager to please.

"That's it. You're the Latin guy I was looking for. You got the job," he said.

PYROTECHNIX

CLIMACTIC FINALE

So it's opening night for *A Junkie for All Seasons*. I'm in my dressing room; a shower curtain's hanging up backstage with a mirror and flashlight. It's sleazy, grimy, and nasty, and I'm getting into character, "The vein, I missed it. I'm jonesing." There's a knock at my shower curtain and Pops walks in. "Hey, open up in there. You're not doing what I think you're doing in there."

"Dad? Hey, Dad, waz up?" I hugged him. "It's great to see ya. You never returned my calls, never wrote, nothing. It's all right. I never took it personally. What brings you here?"

"My new kids wanted to see the show," he said.

"Oh," I said, disappointed.

"My Junior is so much better looking and funny, more talented, more intelligent than you ever were. That's why he's the best in his acting class." Pops beamed proudly.

And I get that look on my face like when you wanna fart without making noise. Pops went on. "I always said if anybody can make something out of nothing, it's you, John. Let's be honest. I know you never liked me."

"I like you, Dad."

"Come on, John, you don't like me," he insisted.

"Dad, you're my father—I gotta like you."

"No, you don't like me. Come on, be a man. Tell me."

"You know, I always thought if I had the father the other kids had, the perfect father, then I wouldn't be so alone. Like when Randy Garcia's father came home their house would fill with laughter. Dad, I'm always waiting for you, waiting for something to be different, waiting for you to be my hero, waiting for you to do one little thing that's gonna help me forgive you. But you always fuck it up."

Or actually I thought I said that; then I realized nothing had come out.

So, he was like, "John. You know I'm not too crazy about you, either. We were never meant to be father and son, but then who the hell really is? We're probably never gonna get along. But that doesn't mean I don't love the shit out of you, even if I can't stand the sight of you. Now go out there and be the best junkie you can be and give me a kiss."

And I thought, "Is that all I am? Is that all I am to you?" And I flashed back to when I saw *A Chorus Line*. Morales wouldn't have been a party to this goddamn spic-ploitation, hustler, junkie, pimp, down-and-outer sucker profanity! The stage manager yelled, "You're on in five." And all of a sudden I allowed myself to want more for myself, to be more and do more, master of my own destiny, never wait for anyone, take life into my own hands, like my father had once wanted for me and like all the Moraleses, Morenos, Arnazes, Puentes, Cheechs and Chongs before me; who had to eat it, live it, get fed up with it, finesse it, scheme it, even Machiavelli it, to get out from under all the ills that Latin flesh is heir to and who dug right down to the bottom of their souls to turn nothing into something. I dedicate this to all of you.

And I think back to sitting with Pops on the fire escape and he says to me again, "Come on, give me a kiss. What are y'fraid of, a little affection?"

"All right, Dad." And I kiss him.

"Not on the lips, you little freak."

And I dedicate this to you, too, Dad.

SPIC-O-RAMA

A DYSFUNCTIONAL COMEDY

JOHN LEGUIZAMO

This text of *Spic-O-Rama* is based on the original one-
man show performed by John Leguizamo. *Spic-O-
Rama* was first produced, but not in its entirety, at the
following theater spaces which are listed with their re-
spective performance dates:

"La Misma Onda (The Same Wave)"—P.S. 122
PERFORMANCES—September 10 & October 8, 1991
CURATOR—Ela Troyano

Gas Station
PERFORMANCES—September 24 & October 3, 4, 16, 24, 1991
ARTISTIC DIRECTOR—Osvaldo Gomariz

Nuyorican Poets Café
PERFORMANCES—October 2, 17 & November 6, 1991
ARTISTIC DIRECTOR—Miguel Algarin

P.S. 122
PERFORMANCES—October 5, 12, 19, 26, 1991
EXECUTIVE DIRECTOR—Mark Russell

Dixon Place
PERFORMANCE—October 18, 1991
ARTISTIC DIRECTOR—Ellie Kovan

Gusto House
PERFORMANCE—November 2, 1991
ARTISTIC DIRECTOR—Andy Kollmorgen

Knitting Factory
PERFORMANCE—November 4, 1991

H.O.M.E. for Contemporary Theatre and Art
PERFORMANCES—November 8, 9, 15, 16, 1991
ARTISTIC DIRECTOR—Randy Rollison

**"Moving Beyond the Madness: A Festival of New Voices"
—New York Shakespeare Festival, Public Theater's
Anspacher Theater**
PERFORMANCE—December 1, 1991
CURATOR—George C. Wolfe
LIGHTING DESIGN—Dan Kotlowitz

On January 16, 1992, *Spic-O-Rama* opened at the Goodman Studio
Theatre in Chicago and was performed in its entirety, which included
slides and videos. It moved to the Briar Street Theatre, again in Chicago, on January 27 and played until March 15. On October 27, 1992,
it opened at New York City's Westside Theatre/Upstairs, where it

ran through January 24, 1993. *Spic-O-Rama* was performed for the last time, in order to be taped for posterity by HBO, at the American Place Theatre in New York City on February 8, 1993.

Goodman Studio Theatre, Chicago
PERFORMANCES—January 14–26, 1992
DIRECTOR—Peter Askin
LIGHTING DESIGN—Ken Bowen
ARTISTIC DIRECTION—Robert Falls
PRODUCTION DIRECTOR—Roche Schulfer
COSTUMES—Theresa Tetley
STAGE MANAGER—Deya S. Friedman
STAGE MANAGER, N.Y.—Michael Robin
The Latino Chicago Theater Company

Briar Street Theatre, Chicago
PERFORMANCES—January 27–March 15, 1992
GENERAL MANAGER—Phil Eickhoff
DIRECTOR—Peter Askin
LIGHTING DESIGN—Ken Bowen
STAGE MANAGER, February—Deya S. Friedman
STAGE MANAGER, March—Michael Robin
MUSIC SUPERVISOR—JellyBean Benitez
COSTUMES—Theresa Tetley
PRODUCTION DIRECTOR—Roche Schulfer
SET DESIGN—Linda Buchanan

Westside Theatre/Upstairs, New York
PERFORMANCES—October 9, 1992–January 24, 1993
DIRECTOR—Peter Askin
SCENIC DESIGN—Loy Arcenas

LIGHTING DESIGNER—Natasha Katz

SOUND DESIGNER—Dan Moses Schreier

VIDEO DESIGN—Dennis Diamond

MUSIC SUPERVISOR—JellyBean Benitez

COSTUME COORDINATOR—Santiago

VIDEO PRODUCTION—Chauncey Street Productions

ASSISTANT STAGE MANAGER—Theresa Tetley

PRODUCERS—Marshall B. Purdy

Michael S. Bregman

Westside Theatre

HBO taping at the American Place Theatre

REHEARSALS—February 5 & 6, 1993

TAPING—February 8, 1993

TV PREMIERE—May 15, 1993

I'd like to dedicate this book to the youth in America (of which I was once one) who have to struggle to live up to so much with so little help and everything in their way.

first encountered John Leguizamo in 1990, while observing an acting class taught by Wynn Handman, director of the American Place Theatre in New York City. John would arrive in class with fragments of what would grow into *Mambo Mouth*, his first one-man show.

A few months later, after I had stopped sitting in on Wynn Handman's class, a friend of mine suggested I go see *Mambo Mouth* at Wynn's Sub-Plot Theatre, which seats about forty people. Now, getting me to go to the theater is about as easy as getting me to go to the public library on New Year's Eve, but I decided to go. In the months to follow I would return to see *Mambo Mouth* fifteen times. "Someone has finally done it," I thought to myself. "This guy has bridged the gap between Richard Pryor and Marlon Brando. He's a phenomenon!"

When John and his director, Peter Askin, asked me to produce *Spic-O-Rama* with them, I was delighted. I had never ventured into theater before, and never will again—unless John wants to do another show.

Since meeting, John and I have collaborated on six projects. He is not only my business associate, he is also my very dear friend.

MICHAEL S. BREGMAN

Producer Michael S. Bregman has made eight films with the Bregman Company. His producing credits include *Betsy's Wedding; Sea of Love; Whispers in the Dark; The Real McCoy* with Kim Basinger and Terence Stamp; *Carlito's Way* with Al Pacino, Sean Penn, John Leguizamo, and Penelope Ann Miller; and the forthcoming *The Shadow* with Alec Baldwin. He is also executive producer of the HBO versions of John Leguizamo's award-winning plays *Mambo Mouth* and *Spic-O-Rama*.

F or a one-man show, *Spic-O-Rama* was huge. It was a
monster. It was, to quote Miggy, "spictacular." For three
months in the dead of winter, it became the hottest ticket
in Chicago. John's phenomenal talent attracted people
of every color and age, from every neighborhood and income. And it
provided the Goodman Theatre with a powerhouse introduction to
Chicago's large and vital Latino community. Quite frankly, I've never
seen anything like it. And *Spic-O-Rama* could have gone on forever.

I became friends with John during his *Mambo Mouth* days, and
late in 1991 (while I was in New York) he took me out to a great salsa
club. He said that he had a new one-man show he'd like to try out as
soon as possible, and he wondered if the Goodman might be inter-
ested. In less than a month, John was performing *Spic-O-Rama* in
our 135-seat Studio Theatre, in association with The Latino Chicago
Theater.

John is miraculously talented, that's a given. But he's also remarkably savvy when it comes to marketing his work. John was in-

terviewed by every Chicago publication and every radio and television station—both English- and Spanish-speaking—and if I read the phrase "born in Bogota, raised in Queens" one more time, I'll lose it. But all that publicity paid off. By the time *Spic-O-Rama* opened—to absolute rave reviews—the publicity had kicked in, word of mouth had taken hold, and the initial two-week run at the Goodman was sold out.

With only two days of downtime, we moved *Spic-O-Rama* to the much larger Briar Street Theatre, where its popularity exploded. It was *the* show to see. It achieved cult status with a segment of Chicago theatergoers who returned time after time to see Miggy and his dysfunctional Gigante family, and it continued to draw a large Latino audience every night—at least forty percent by John's own estimate. *Spic-O-Rama* sold out its initial two-week run at the Briar Street in no time, was extended for another two weeks, and if John hadn't had other commitments, would probably still be running there today.

Spic-O-Rama was one of those extraordinary experiences that reaffirm your faith in your craft, your art. Its message was universal, and its heart was the blazing talent, boundless energy, and unfailing decency of its creator, John Leguizamo. I speak for the entire Goodman staff when I say that working with John (and with everyone he brought with him—Peter, Theresa, Robin, et al.) was sheer joy. For three months we all became hip-hop junkies. So, in the immortal words of the youngest Gigante, "'M, to the 'I' to the 'G, G, Y' go Miggy!"

ROBERT FALLS

Robert Falls has been the artistic director of the Goodman Theatre since 1986, after serving in that capacity at Chicago's Wisdom Bridge Theatre from 1977 to 1985. His Goodman directing credits include

The Iceman Cometh, Galileo, Landscape of the Body, Pal Joey, the world premiere of *The Speed of Darkness, The Misanthrope, Book of the Night*, and most recently, the world premieres of *On the Open Road* and *Riverview: A Melodrama with Music*. Additional directing credits include productions for the Guthrie Theater, Chicago's Remains Theatre, the La Jolla Playhouse, and Broadway. Mr. Falls most recently directed *The Iceman Cometh* for the Abbey Theatre in Dublin, Ireland, and *On the Open Road* at the New York Shakespeare Festival.

'm sitting here with John Leguizamo in a funky psychedelic Mexican eatery, El Poco Loco, translation: "The Little Crazy." That's just what it's been like these couple of hours—with the vibrant and festive colors on every wall and artifact, the loud *fat* beat kicking out of the speakers, and the sumptuous repast before us, I feel as if I'm inside some giant's fecund mind. And the little giant, John, is dressed in his finest hip-hop-bad-boy garb, spewing hyperkinetically between mouthfuls of Mexican nouvelle cuisine for the nouveau riche.

So here we are. I'll try to make this short and painful. Now, how did you start writing *Spic-O-Rama,* your second one-person thang? What was your first impulse?

It was March and I was six months into performing *Mambo Mouth* off-Broadway at the American Place Theatre and I needed some form of distraction. Some kind of new challenge. I kept changing the show *(Mambo)* but it wasn't enough for me. Until one day I saw a guy on the street in Desert Storm fatigues just hanging on the street corner with his boom box. It was *Waiting for Godot* Latino-fied. Then I let him live in my mind, trying to figure out what he did for a living, what he would sound like. Then I remembered all my friends who went into the service and a whole new character came out—Krazy Willie. I started improvising and putting on his military wardrobe. He came to life. Then his story started to tell itself and from his story the other characters emerged.

Why another one-man show? Why not a full play? Didn't you have enough the first time?

What are you, a critic? Where do you get off not thinking it's a full-length play? It's a Latin *Long Day's Journey into Night,* but comic.

Yes, I appreciate that literary allusion, but try not to digress. Look, what I mean is, how is it a play as opposed to a series of loosely strung monologues?

I wanted to do something very different from *Mambo Mouth.* I still wanted the one-man-solo-monologue format, because it was a form I loved and admired. I feel it's the oldest form of storytelling. The most organic. It's the first man—Cretaceous or Jurassic—sitting around the fire chewing on a brontosaurus leg and retelling the day's events and acting them out. And I'm sure he was a smartass who made fun of everyone and got some handouts for being amusing or maybe they stoned him to death.

Peter (director and confidant) Askin also wanted to challenge me and take my writing to the next level, a more interconnected story instead of the random vignettes of *Mambo Mouth*. The story as a whole has unity and momentum moving toward an event: the wedding.

.

Yes, a plot! Thank God for a unifying theme or a little structure to sink your crowns on. Now, tell me, what other elements make *Spic-O-Rama* different from *Mambo Mouth*?

As I changed costumes and prepared for each new scene in *Mambo Mouth*, the audience saw the silhouette of someone dancing behind a screen. In *Spic-O-Rama* we replaced the silhouette with videos that keep the forward motion accelerating. The videos bridged the plot and also aided in camouflaging the costume changes which, with Theresa Tetley *(Mambo Mouth* silhouette bar none), we had down to between one and a half minutes (on the slow side) and forty-five seconds (our quickest). That's if everything went right, which it often didn't. Many a time, I came out with an open zipper or without Gladyz's wig or forgetting to tuck my nether regions into the spandex.

The videos provided a break from the one-man monotony and added a new voice and flavor. Seeing the people the characters in the show referred to deepened the whole experience. For example: Vanna Blanca, Javier's dominatrix girlfriend, explains to little Miggy what she does for a living: "I'm an escort. I escort people. It's like your mother. She gives you candy to go to the supermarket with her and . . . you . . . escort her to the market. And she'll give you candy or something for going. That's what I do."

And on men: "They need to be spanked on a regular basis. Unless they like it, of course."

Let's talk about your personal life.

Let's not.

Well, what I mean is how much of *Spic-O-Rama* came from your personal life? [John sits very stoically, making origami machine guns with his napkins. I'm sensitive. I pick up the subtle clues and move on.]

Okay, you knew this one was coming: Why the title? Was it for the controversy? Inquiring minds want to know.

What do you mean? What's so controversial about Rama, the ancient Egyptian god?

Don't try to skirt the issue, you little avoidance demon. I'm talking about the *S* word—spic. Why spic?

Plain good old-fashioned unadulterated controversy. I like the shocking and the raw. It's something that thrills me. It was daring and a bit offputting, and that's exactly why I liked it. Hence, *Spic-O-Rama*.

That's a nice pat answer, but really, what's the story behind the title?

Thank you for putting me in my place, Digression Police. Yes, the title's vicious because it represents overcoming the evils of life. The play is all told from a little boy's perspective and the little boy was me in a lot of ways.

Let me tell you, being called a spic at the age of nine was a total shock. We lived in a part of Queens that was just turning Hispanic and a lot of the remaining families were white trash. (See! Hispanics are like the cleaning bacteria at the bottom of the food chain. We move into neighborhoods that are dying and change them into something more lively and festive. We're like mushrooms [fungi]—beneficial to the cycle of renewal.)

So anyway, I was very friendly with the white-trash families (I had no choice—they were the only kids on the block). And whenever there was an argument back then, the swearing would turn to, "You spics, get out of my block! You're ruining the neighborhood." (Yeah, like we kept them from renovating. We held their hands back from painting their stoops and we hid their pens so they couldn't fill out job applications. Give me a break!) But that word would turn up time and time again and it affects your formative years—creates toxic shame. It pulls you right out of the moment and you say to yourself, "Damn! I didn't know I was a spic. How come my parents never told me? Yeah, I look different. But different is good, isn't it?"

The title also took something heinous and made it benign. Rendered a weapon harmless. Detonated a bomb. I'm from the Lenny Bruce and Richard Pryor school of thinking: If you use a word often enough, it loses its meaning and value. Richard Pryor used the word *nigger* in most of the titles of his works to reappropriate its negative effect. He took control of it.

The title was screaming for attention in a medium where we are not represented. Latinos are at least ten percent of the population of the United States—that's 26 million Latinos—but nowhere present in the media. So I figured I'd use a title that screamed, "Hey, someone's ignoring us. Why are we being ignored? Is there a subliminal curse on us? Are we carrying some stigma?" So naturally, *Spic-O-Rama* seemed important.

However, the title did give me trouble down the line. Without having seen the show, some Chicago news stations would not have anything to do with the play and Canada refused to air the HBO version

solely based on the title. They wouldn't even look at it. And some Latino intelligentsia were like, "There he goes again, our prodigal son,
denigrating us. We had such hope for him." If they missed the boat
once, they'll miss it twice. If they didn't get *Mambo Mouth*, they won't
get *Spic-O-Rama*.

Why a dysfunctional family? How did you arrive at this motley crew?

I picked a family—well, actually, the family in the play adopted me.
Some of the most important theater works, masterpieces, have been
about families, and almost all are semi-demi-autobiographical. They
reveal the most and touch me the most. *Long Day's Journey into Night*
and *Death of a Salesman* are my top two favorites. So I set out to create a comic tragic family that is closer to the way I perceive the world.
Sort of funny and painful at the same time.

The family is where it all begins. It's what forms and drives us
for the rest of our lives. *Oedipus, Hamlet*—you name the classic hero.
Look at *Ordinary People*. We all have some wretched inner child who's
angry or resentful or traumatized, and that is what drives us for the
rest of our lives. No one is exempt.

**What is your "process?" Do you test your material out? I mean, well,
the question is more about development of the entire play from the
germ of an idea, so to speak. Come on, give it up.**

I always write my work down, go over a few drafts, and then my mad
experiment begins. It always begins in a living room with tons of
coffee and some appetizers to keep the audience of family and close
friends awake and eager through these marathon all-night events. I
read these twenty-page character monologues, giving them only a
few intermissions to recaffeinate. Then the comments begin. I usu-

ally can't help but antagonize anyone with a negative comment. But I have to protect myself, don't I? I'm right, aren't I? I start arguing back and defending my work, but they're used to it. Well, at least I am.

Then I go furiously to work. Get notes from Peter and cut and restructure.

There are a lot of writers who find it difficult to kill their darlings: precious bits, lines, and moments that they have spent years refining and can't find it in their hearts to cut. Is it difficult for you to edit your material?

No. My idea of cutting is to enlarge the margins and reduce the font. So the appearance of cutting is achieved and my little progeny will not be eviscerated. But Pierre (that's French for Peter) catches on and I have to reduce the script, usually by half. A process that feels like someone is cutting off an appendage.

When do you know you're ready? When to stop cutting? Does an editing fairy come in the night and take away your red pen?

Well, it never stops changing. That's the beauty of theater to me. It keeps evolving. I can improve it every night. Acting, writing, timing, lighting—everything.

But you digress. At this stage of my "process" I usually invite more friends for more coffee and more crudités. I'm still just reading from the script at this point because I don't want the focus to be on my acting but on the words and the story. And when I take away the script, my acting distracts from just what is written down. It's harder on the audience, but hey, what are friends for?

Then I'm ready to take it to the downtown clubs. I take my props and three or four of the characters at first and start to build from there. Don't wanna shoot my wad all at once. Usually my brother, Sergio, or Theresa Tetley or Michael Robin (stage manager for both *Mambo Mouth* and *Spic-O-Rama*) help me schlep across town with projector and costumes en suite.

Where are these enclaves of fermenting creativity?

First destination is downtown in the lesser-known and smaller venues (less audience, less criticism). I'm still vulnerable and must keep nurturing my work, even though I have quite a callus on my soul from doing improv and sketch comedy. The places I go to (thank God I'm in New York, the mecca of performance art spaces) are Dixon Place, the Gas Station, P.S. 122, Nuyorican Poets Café, and H.O.M.E. for Contemporary Theatre and Art.

And then I'm ready for a lot more rewrites and restructuring. Peter and I set appointments, break them, and rework the whole sucker. He helps and guides me. I stubbornly stick to my offspring and he plays along, knowing in the back of his head he'll get his way eventually. It's a perfect synergy. Peter and I are a perfectly complementary team. He's great with structure and my strength is dialogue and character.

You took the play to the Goodman Theatre in Chicago, where you performed it for the first time in its entirety. How did you get it there and how had it changed from the downtown clubs?

Well, it's a romantic story. I was performing a version of it at the H.O.M.E. and my caring, trusting, loving agent, David Lewis, invited Robert Falls (artistic director of the Goodman) to come and witness one of my readings. It was love at first sight. But like any relationship, demands and expectations get set up. And Bob (I can call him that) felt the story needed some tweaking. So Pedro (that's Spanish for Peter) and I mind-melded and restructured. The plot changed drastically, from being Raffi's wedding to Krazy Willie's wedding, which then made Krazy the main character and Raffi the other brother.

The videos we talked about earlier were finally added. We shot them with some old colleagues, Chauncey Street Productions, who had done a bang-up job with a special for the Comedy Channel called *The Talent Pool.* I used a lot of the actors from a comedy workshop I started and some kids from public schools. Picked the best of the bunch and they proved to be a wonderful addition. You just give them the material and let them paraphrase and improvise around it and you get gems—for example: In the video following Miggy's monologue, Eurasia says on the subject of family, "You can have a lot of fathers, but you have only one mother."

Some of the other videos were just interviews and yet others were elaborately set up, like the wedding, which was intercut with actual footage from a Bronx wedding.

How did it keep changing?

Lines kept improving. The whole fight between Miggy, the white kid, and Ivan was first a checkers fight and after the first month became a spitting contest. More jokes came to mind. "See, you don't have to go to a third-world country to adopt me. I'm right here" was added shortly before opening night. My acting kept loosening up: Raffi became more flamboyant, Gladyz more vivacious, the father more bitter.

All except one piece improved. The one exception was a monologue, which I dedicated to my brother, about a physically challenged man. It came easily and effortlessly at first, especially in Chicago because I had just finished the three months of readings and was right on schedule in the "process." But on the reopening in New York and for about two months into the off-Broadway performance I struggled. I couldn't connect with the content until the last few weeks of the run. Then, out of exhaustion, I just gave in to the piece and let it take me wherever and it became something quite wonderful on its own.

What was the reaction from the public in Chicago?

We did the play for two weeks at the Goodman's smaller space which had about 135 seats. The two weeks were sold out before we opened with a waiting list of 600 people and phones ringing off the hook. This was all due to the *Mambo Mouth* airing on HBO and the Goodman's tapping, for the first time, into the huge Hispanic population of Chicago which was mostly Mexican and Puerto Rican with a smattering of Colombians and Cubans.

Do you have a system? A regime? I mean, how do you prepare for such an arduously physical task as a play?

I started running daily and working out like a fiend. I needed the aerobic endurance for this 105-minute show that could grow even longer, depending on the laughs. (Our longest show in Chicago ran 119 minutes, almost two hours.) And I had an ulterior motive—I wanted to look good in Gladyz's tights and midriff.

We then moved to the 400-seat Briar Street Theatre. By this time, the reviews were coming out and they were exceptional. The consensus was in: Chicago would be our second home. The audiences were highly responsive—white, Hispanic, and black. The *Tribune* wrote a piece on the show talking about the multiethnic audience, teenagers on dates, the upper echelons of theatergoers in furs—it was like an ad for Benetton.

I got many dinner invites, offers to live with families, and the usual "What are you doing tonight?" (wink wink nudge nudge). I also got material gifts like jackets and what-not. (See! Celebrity does have its positive side.) But Nancy Reagan got in trouble for that, so I make sure I pay tax on those suckers.

Some people came with pots of homemade food—*arroz con gandules* (rice with pigeon peas), Puerto Rican soul food, *pudin*, etc. I was invited to try the many Colombian restaurants' ample menus. I always brought Theresa Tetley and Michael Robin. We had done *Mambo Mouth* together and we were doing *Spic-O-Rama* together and enjoying the success. If you don't have close friends to steal some of the credit, who can you enjoy your success with?

The mayor and governor declared March 15, 1992, to be John Leguizamo Day. That one day was like out of *The Wizard of Oz*. A proclamation was given unto me and I instantly felt I had . . . *(SINGS)* a brain, a heart . . . the nerve.

How did a hardened, inner-city New Yorker like yourself fare out in the mild-mannered Midwest?

I was suspicious of everyone's goodness and kindness (an old New York tendency). I kept thinking they're too nice—they must be up to something!

Why did you wait five months between the Chicago and New York productions?

I went to shoot *Super Mario Brothers* and returned five months later.

I had to work hard to get back into the physical and emotional life of the play, because for some reason I didn't want to go to that bitter, angry place within myself. But I got it toward the last weeks before we closed.

What was it like bringing it back to New York?

I expected the worst from the reviewers in New York.

Why? They loved *Mambo Mouth*.

Everyone knows that after you've had one success they come at you much harder and expect more from you and try to crush you the second time. (I'm not paranoid!) I learned early on from other actors not to let reviews affect me, but you can't help but get affected. So I prepared for the worst and hoped for the best.

I saw your show in Chicago, and in New York I noticed that you changed the ending. Why did you do that? Are you an obsessive-compulsive perfectionist?

I was having a Dostoevskian episode trying to figure out the ending of the last piece of the play and it simply wouldn't come. It just lay there and sucked. We tried everything. Shortening it. Lengthening it. Saying it quicker. But it kept sucking.

Petrovich (Russian for Peter) was never happy with the ending of the play either. He felt it didn't quite close the story and leave the audience with a bang. We were toiling away constantly trying to improve it. Then he thought of ending it with something I had written for Miggy but could never find a place for, about his disgruntledness toward God, and boom—it fit and the show had an ending.

I heard you were trying to get the show at the Public. What happened?

We had tentative dates set for the Public. We were trying to do a Good-man and N.Y.S.F. collaboration. George C. Wolfe wanted the show and Joanne Akalaitis didn't. The talks went on and then I got *Super Mario Brothers* (which paid an incredible lot and eventually provided the money that produced *Spic-O-Rama*), so I went with it.

I worked on *Mario* from May to August. When I got back, the Public was no longer available. I had a few offers to take *Spic-O-Rama* to Broadway, but doing that meant giving the film rights away and doing eight performances a week for what I was sure would have been a minimum of six months with a condition to extend. And that kind of a lucky break was a bit of a problem. My instrument (if I may be so artsy) couldn't take it. During *Mambo Mouth* I went to several voice therapists. Changed my diet. No fried food or spicy food. No smoking. No caffeine. No drinking. No grunting during sex. The life of the ascetic was mine. To repeat this again gets tougher as you get older.

Even though I was miked, the physical demands of *Spic-O-Rama* always left me completely drained and hoarse. My methody self would start preparing at three p.m. for an eight p.m. show, so my voice would be raspy and my throat burned after every perfor-mance. The cumulative effect would make my voice get raspier and raspier as time went on. To do only four months and maybe six per-formances a week—all I could stand physically—was not a profit-able enticement to producers, especially since Peter and I wanted the tickets to be as affordable as possible so that lower-income folk could make it.

It ended up that I became one of the producers along with the Westside Theatre and Michael S. Bregman (who went above and beyond the call of duty). I was scared, but I put the money I had just painfully earned on *Super Mario Brothers* into my own work because I believed in it. To be honest, though, the chances of getting my money back looked grim.

The show opened. We sold out all the previews to audiences which, surprisingly, were made up of eighty percent Latinos. Then the reviews came out and business doubled and we sold out the whole run. We nearly doubled our investment. Life is sweet.

What was the audience response?

Again what happened in Chicago. Offers from fans. I got Playbills with lipstick kisses and telephone numbers. Letters about the best sex I would ever get. Tempting. More material rewards, gifts: Some fans gave me cups engraved with *Spic-O-Rama*, towels with my name monogrammed, etc.

Did you ever get tired or bored doing it night after night for four months?

No, I kept finding new laughs. Better ways of saying certain things. I would ad-lib new jokes during performances. Peter also kept coming up with new and better ways of saying lines that made the show tighter and funnier. And he kept me fine-tuned like a lead guitar. The show got a little soft around the third month of the New York run. Like a comfortable pair of shoes.

Previews, by far, were the most exciting. But every now and then I had a great performance. Sometimes, it's just one character that really shines. But it's always up for grabs. Even though I prepare, things happen to me. Each audience has its own personality, which affects me. If I had a bad day and was angry, it would be an angrier show. If something tragic happened that day, my performance would reflect that. That's what makes theater the most incredible kind of performance art. It's the most honest. On film you do take after take until you finally feel the right emotion or they can cut away from you if you just don't get it and infer it another way. But onstage the audience knows if you're there or if you're faking it.

And the things that go wrong make it a thrilling challenge. Gladyz was a real hazard—boobs kept falling down, her wig tangled on a nail on the set; I burned myself on the cigarettes, choked on the food. Once Gladyz pushed the carriage too hard by accident, overturning it, killing the baby, and spilling out all the props, which almost rolled off the stage. Krazy Willie's shirt got caught on the fence and for all my pulling, I couldn't free myself. Can you believe it—right in the middle of my most passionate lines! So I began to act like I was having a flashback, "All right, I'll give my serial number. Let go. I don't have any secrets," then ad-libbed, "I hate when that happens."

When I was there I saw Madonna. Who else attended?

I'm not name-dropping, I'm downright bragging. My idol, De Niro, came on the last performance. Came down to my dressing room. And in his most De Niroish way, which is very economical, congratulated me. (Another dream come true. See, visualizing works!) Martin Short, Brian Di Palma (couldn't get Coppola in, much to my chagrin), Mike Nichols who wrote me a very funny letter, Jodie Foster, Nathan Lane, the king of one-man shows, Eric Bogosian. See, this spic has pull, baby.

How did you prepare for the HBO taping?

We had to cut the script to fit the 55-minute requirement without los-ing the JPMs (jokes per minute). We lost Javier and the closing we had struggled so hard to get right. Had to include the camera angles into the performance—when I would look into the camera, when not to, that sort of thing.

How was the filming different from a regular performance stage?

The smaller audience, the smaller laughs. I had a fever and a cold. I'd been away from the material for about two weeks and had to get in the groove very quickly. We had four cameras rolling and the camera operators talked often and loudly, which is tough when you're used to just hearing yourself talk. Distractions of film changes, commands from the booth. Lights not working, the cameras going down during the show, etc.

It must be hard to be both writer and actor?

I don't know how Orson Welles and Woody Allen do it. They direct, write, and star in their own productions. It's tough switching hats. As the writer, it's one mind-set, and as an actor I have to reapproach the material totally fresh. Acting someone else's material is a million times less formidable.

What do you feel is the basic difference between TV, live theater, and film?

Theater is the actor's medium, film the director's, and TV the pro-ducer's. Onstage it's you, by yourself. No one is going to save you by yelling "Cut!" or letting you do ten takes till you get it right. You're either in the moment or you're not. Which is really ideal, since you learn to respect yourself and leave yourself alone. Live performance is still the most organic of all the media. Because it's not done with machines or editing, it's got all the imperfections, all the mistakes, and all the magic of real talent.

El Fin

GLOSSARY OF

FOREIGN TERMS

amigos y socios: friends and colleagues

asqueroso: disgusting slime

Ay, fo!: Euuu, yuck, p.u., it stinks, nasty

babas: dribble, spit

bendito: poor thing, blessèd

Bien nice y chévere: Real nice and groovy, kool

blanca: white (feminine)

bobo: jerk (masculine)

boricua: Puerto Rican. Derived from the Indian name for the island

bruja: witch (feminine)

cabeza: head (both literal and sexual meanings)

cabróncito: little motherfucker (masculine)

chaito: good-bye

chichichita: my little poopsie, my little bubeleh

cobarde: coward

condenado: weasel (masculine)

coño: damn, shit, fuck, piss, etc.

culo: butt, asshole

desgraciada: wretch (but stronger, with more disgust; feminine)

Dios mío!: My God!

Epa! Epa!: Groove it! Groove it!

Et tu: (Latin) And you (from *Julius Caesar:* "Et tu, Brute?")

Et voilà, mon frères!! Je suis ici: (Imperfect French) And look, my brothers!! Here I am

felicitaciónes: congratulations

gigante: giant

gordita: chubbikins (feminine)

guevón: big stupid bonehead

Hola: Hello

Imaginate!: Imagine that!

inútil: useless

jodona: kvetcher, annoying person (feminine)

la majadera: the rube (feminine)

las feitas: the ugly ones (feminine)

las morenitas: the dark-skinned ones (feminine)

las negritas: the black ones (feminine)

loca: crazy (feminine)

malparido: abomination

maricón: a pejorative for one who indulges in same-sex love

matrimonio: matrimony

Me cago en tu madre: I shit on your mother

Menealo!: Move it!

Metale semilla a la maraca pa que suene: Put the seeds in the maraca so it will go

Me tiene: He has me

mija: my daughter, my darling

mijo: my son, my darling

mira: look

Mira el mutant: Look at the mutant

mondongo: tripe (a Spanish delicacy non-Latinos find quite heinous—litmus test for true Latinoness)

mujeriando: wenching

muy: very, extremely

nada: nothing

nena(s): girlfriend(s)

niña: girl

No invente papito: Don't play me

No joda: Don't be annoying. Give me a break

No joda zángano, lo cojo y lo vuelvo mierda. Le hago que le salgan plátanos por el culo: Don't bother me, rascal, I'll catch you and beat the shit out of you. I'll make plantains come out of your butt

Oye, cómo va?: Hey, how's it going?

papá: endearment to loved ones (masculine)

papi: endearment used by parents; e.g.: little pops (masculine)

pendeja: dummy (feminine)

pendejo: dummy (masculine)

Pero, ojo: But, careful

por favor: please

porqué: because

Porqué tú me haz jodido y no puedo más. Y no es mi culpa: Because you have fucked me and I can't take any more. And it's not my fault

porquería: trash

Pues claro: But of course

puta: whore

Puta(s) sucia(s): nasty dirty whore(s)

Que Dios me haga más vieja antes de mi tiempo: May God make me older before my time

Qué embustera: What a deceiver

Qué linda: How pretty

Qué mentirosa: What a liar (feminine)

Qué precioso: How handsome

Qué rico!: How tasty!

Qué te pasa, nenita?: What'sa matter with you, baby?

Qué's eso?: What's that?

Regarde: (French) Observe

Sabrosito!: Delicious!

Sana que sana, culito de rana (si no sana hoy, sañara manana): Heal, heal, little toad-butt; if you don't heal today, you will tomorrow

santera: a witch doctor or shaman (feminine)

Santería: a religious practice in Latin American countries taken from African voodoo, native South American folklore, and European Catholicism (it works, for a small fee)

Sí, es sad, verdad. El primero, tú sabes: Yes, it's sad, right. The first one, you know how it is

Tan bonita la niña. Tan preciosa. Ay tenía que ser mia: So pretty the little girl. So precious, oh she had to be mine

Tú eres un maricón, malparido y guevón: You are a faggot, abomination, and have some nerve

Tú lo mereces: You deserve it

Tú sabes: You know

una enema grandisima!: a huge enema!

Un sinvergüenza: A wise guy

verdad?: right?

yo debo: I oughtta

zángano: rascal (masculine)

GLOSSARY OF

SLANG TERMS

axed: asked

be the flavor: be the star of the situation

buggin': getting mad, going crazy (e.g.: "He's buggin'" as in "He must be crazy")

burnouts: homeys, fellas, posse of worn-out potheads and whatnot; losers

coochie: buttocks, gluteus maximus, tush

dissed: disrespected

dogging: do something bad like cheat on people, disregard them

fesses: confesses

fugly: contraction for fucking ugly

gonna: going to

gotta: got to

ho: whore

homey, homes, homeslice, G, B: forms of "homeboy," used by Chicanos in jail in the fifties to mean "from my hometown," appropriated by African-Americans in the eighties and by everyone else in the nineties

I'mma school her: I'm going to teach her

in the house: when someone is ruling the scene, someone makes an appearance or is guesting

kick it back: answer back

Lookaher: Look at her

musta: must have

sex up: to have sex with

shout out: make a toast to, dedication

skankless: without filthiness

skeeze: to sleaze, sleep around

smokin': hot

suckerbutt: smells like a butt, looks like a butt, is a butt

This is the shit!: This is what's happening!

Waz up?: What's up?

weasel: cheat, act sneaky or snaky, get one's way underhandedly, be very Machiavellian (e.g.: Nixon weaseled in the White House)

wichoo: with you

word: form of agreement (e.g.: A: "She was fly!" B: "Word!"); that's the truth; really

youse: all of you

"There is no greatness without a passion to be great, whether it's the aspiration of an athlete or an artist, a scientist, a parent or a businessman."

—*Anthony Robbins's Personal Power!*

Success Journal Volume 3, Cassette 1, Days 5–7

(Audience and stage are completely dark. Rap music sounds in the background and we hear the voices of children at play in a school yard. Miggy leaps onto the stage and appears to fly through the air as he dances hard, lit by a strobe light which catches him in midair when he jumps. After the adrenaline of the audience is pumped by this seemingly impossible stunt, the lights come up and we see nine-year-old Miggy wearing a long blue stocking cap, thick translucent blue glasses, teeth with overbite, Day-Glo orange oversized jeans, yellow-and-blue flannel shirt buttoned to the top, and high-top sneakers. Miggy is standing center stage with a row of industrial-yellow-colored dryers on his left, a chain-link fence with a beat-up old car parked behind him at center stage, and a bed with a white-framed window to its side on his right.)

MIGGY: *(To his teacher, at rear of audience:)* What?? What?!! But Mister Gabrielli, I've had my report ready—you just never axed me. *(Pulls down screen for slides. Under breath:)* Suckerbutt. *(To Mr. Gabrielli:)* I didn't say nothing.

(To class/audience:) "Monsters, Freaks, and Weirdos," by Miguel Gigante. My science fair project is loosely based on my family. And any similarities are just purely on purpose.

(Aside to a nearby classmate:) I can too do it on my family. I can do my project on anything I want, welfare face.

(To class:) My *(Looks at scribbling on his hand.)* hypothecus will prove, class of 501, that no child should have to put up with the evil inhumanation that I live with every day. Especially a nine-year-old genius with the potential of myself. *(Pats himself on the back. Aside to same classmate:)* You're just jealous cause you live in the projects. *(Sings:)* Your father is in jail, your brother's out on bail, and your mother is a ho!

(To class:) Last year I axed Santa Claus for a normal regular family, but I guess I must be punished for something I don't even know

what I did. So I got all these mutants for family. And at exactly five
o'clock, carloads of the most nastiest freakazoids are gonna come to
my house for my brother's wedding and so I'mma run away and the
next time you see me I'm gonna be on the back of a carton of chocolate milk. *(Aside:)* Shut up! I'm getting to it. Oh, my God, I'm sorry,
Mister Gabrielli! I didn't know it was you. How was I supposed to
know it was you? I didn't smell your breath. *(Digs in his butt as he
turns on slide projector and approaches screen.)* Okay . . . What?

(To class:) This is me, of course. With my handsome pre-Columbian
features. See, you don't have to go to a third-world country to adopt
me, I'm right here!

This is my brother, Krazy Willie. We call him crazy cause he is. I share my room with him and this is his fake homemade Soloflex. *(Runs to stage right, which is decorated as a boy's bedroom. Jumps up on the single bed, then jumps to reach chin-up bar hanging from the ceiling. Does one pull-up and counts out loud:)* Eight, nine, ten. *(Then drops to bed, leaps off bed, and runs back to center stage.)*

He went to Desert Storm and it's the most important thing he's done in his life. But my father still calls him a loser. He's getting married tonight and I'm not gonna have anybody to protect me no more. Word. Cause he lets me hang out with him and watch him get high and sex up the females. *(Maniacal giggles.)*

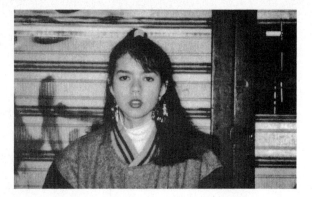

This is his female, Yvonne. He calls women females so he don't get confused. And this proud eleventh grader can be seen at Show World nightly.

These are his burnouts. That's Chewey and that's Boulevard. Waz up? Waz up?

This is his sex mobile. Someone stole the motor so it don't work, so they just hang in there and pretends to go places.

This is my other brother, Raffi—brains not included. I have to share my room with him, too. And I don't dislike him. I just hate him intensely. Cause if he's not talkin' about himself, he's talkin' to himself. And he's weird, cause he thinks he's white. *(To random audience member:)* Oh, yeah, even whiter than you, mister! *(To class:)* Word. One day, he locked himself in our room for hours and hours. And when he finally came out, he was screaming, "Look, look! A miracle, a miracle! The most sacred lady of Flushing has appeared before me, transforming me into an albino white person." And he has blond hair and blue eyes. Na-ah! Na-ah! Not even. Cause I searched our room and found that miracle—holy water by Saint Clorox.

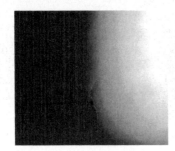

This is my other brother, Javier. He didn't let me take a picture of him so all I got was a picture of his finger. And he don't live with us cause he's like those freaks and monsters they keep in dungeons and broom closets and they scream and yell and live off of bugs— that's him. He's my brother, but it's not my fault cause you don't pick 'em, you just get 'em, and sometimes they come out irregular like Javier.

Oh, guess who else is coming to the wedding. My bugged-out aunt Ofelia. She became a santera—that's a black magic healer—cause she couldn't get no dates! Word, she's got magical powers. I'm serious. Look into her eyes. Oooh, you're getting sleepy. Oooh, you're getting sleepy. *(Slide goes in and out of focus.)* You are under my power. Take off your clothes, everybody! *(To Mr. Gabrielli:)* I was just playing, Mister Gabrielli. *(Under breath:)* Suckerbutt.

Eeeuuu! That's my uncle, Brother Gonzales. He makes me call him Uncle Brother. He's a really mean evil guy who loves money. So he charges for confession. Look, watch this. *(Addresses slide:)* Oh, Uncle Brother? Oh, Uncle Brother? I'm here for confession. What is this? *(Pulls dollar bill from pocket.)* It looks like a dollar. Look at him come after it. Come on, you greedy pig, come and get it.

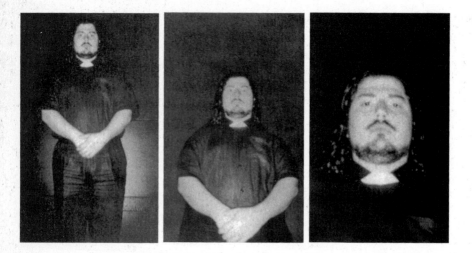

See, I learned how to work that religion thing this summer.

This is my cousin, Efraim. I can't show you him cause he's an illegal alien, all right?

(Quickly passes to next slide.)

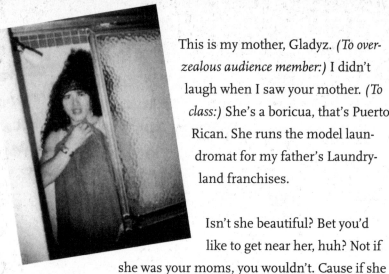

This is my mother, Gladyz. *(To over-zealous audience member:)* I didn't laugh when I saw your mother. *(To class:)* She's a boricua, that's Puerto Rican. She runs the model laundromat for my father's Laundryland franchises.

Isn't she beautiful? Bet you'd like to get near her, huh? Not if she was your moms, you wouldn't. Cause if she was your moms she'd make you read the encyclopedia before you go to bed every night. And I have to finish volumes M to T before I get my Christmas present, which I don't even want cause I know it's going to be more encyclopedias. My mother says she's doing it because she loves me. Well, I don't know if love can kill, but it's getting real close.

This is my father, Felix. He's Colombian. *(To classmate:)* What did you call my father? Mister Gabrielli, he called my father a drug dealer. *(To classmate:)* I'mma kick your ass. I'll take care of it, Mister Gabrielli. *(To audience member as if student in class:)* Did you ever kiss a rabbit between the ears? *(Pulls his pockets out.)* Go ahead. Kiss it. Kiss it. You asked for it, stupid. Stupid! *(Mumbles curses under breath and sucks teeth as he returns to center stage.)*

We have to live with my uncle and Aunt Ofelia so we can pay rent, cause my father takes all the money that should be ours and he gives it to his nasty girlfriends. Now can you guess which is his most favorite nasty girlfriend?

Is it Enigma?

Or Eutopia?

Or is it Yolanda?

I think it's the one with the guilty sweaty pits. *(Points to Yolanda's armpit.)* Aha!!

(Turns slide projector off.) I'm not supposed to tell you this, I'm not supposed to tell you this. You can't make me! You can't make me! All right, you win! I'm gonna tell you anyway. My mother was going through my father's pants and she found a letter from Yolanda. So she set all my father's pants on fire. *(Walks to stage left, set up as laundromat, and removes burned pair of shorts from one of the machines. Shows audience, then throws back into machine, slams door, and returns to center stage.)* And my father came home and caught her and called her "la negra india puta inmunda del carajo"—"the nastiest black Indian ho of hell." And my mother cursed right back, "Tú eres un maricón, malparido y guevón." Look it up! And my father smacked my moms *(Mimes.)*, so she ran and told my grandmother and my grandmother said, "Bueno, tú lo mereces"—"Good, you deserve it"—in her nasty parrot voice. And my mother gave her the evil "Chupame la teta!"—"Suck my titty!" And my grandmother reslapped my moms. *(Mimes all action.)* And my mom jumped on her and started choking her and then my father came into the room and grabbed my mom in a half-nelson and I jumped on him and started kickin' him and punchin' him and kickin' him *(Starts having an asthma attack.)* and he pushed me off and told me, "Go to your room and mind your

business." So I went to my room. *(Walks to bedroom, stage right, and sits on foot of bed.)* Cause I got a headache, like when you drink milk too fast. And I knew they were going to kill themselves and I didn't want to hear it, so I just closed my eyes and put my fingers in my ears. *(Stands up, eyes closed, fingers in ears, and dances, singing:)*

> Who's in the house?
> Miggy's in the house.
> "M" to the "I" . . . *(Changes tempo.)*
> Nice and smooth and funky,
> I'm a hip-hop junkie.
> All I wanna do is hm hm to you
> *(Pelvic thrust.)*

And when I pulled my fingers out of my ears and opened up my eyes, my father had moved out.

And I'mma miss him. Especially when he's drunk. Cause when he's drunk—oh, my God, he becomes the nicest man in the world. And he hugs me and kisses me and tells me that I'm his favorite son. And he begins to cry and cry and pulls out his maracas and tells how he almost played with Carlos Santana. Oh, my God, it's so much fun.

Then every holiday, I take all my savings and wait outside of Liquor World until I find somebody to buy me a big bottle of Colt 45 as a present for my father.

(Turns projector back on.) Okay, this is the last shout out. This is the last skankless shout out and it goes to: my homes, my partner . . . Ivan!

(Chants:) Go chubby. Go chubby. Get stupid. Get stupid. Buggin' out y'all! Come on, stand up, Ivan, don't be shy. Me and Ivan are real close cause we came up with this game at the Fresh-Air Fund camp this summer.

Cause look how much fun we're having. So we came up with this game—spit basketball, where everyone had to spit in a bucket and the first person to get twenty-one won. And this big kid came along all uninvited and pushed Ivan, so I had to play him. And I beat him. And I don't know what came over him, cause all I said was, "I murdelized you. I destroyed you. Miggy's in the house!" And the sore loser picked up the bucket and poured it all over me and said, "Get out of my country, you stupid ugly spic!" Now I could of beat him up so bad, cause when you're angry, oh, my God, you can beat up people who are a million zillion trillion times your size.

But I didn't do nothing. Cause I didn't want to act like it counted. So I just stared at the kid and said, "Yes, yes, yes, I *am* a spic. I'm . . . I'm spic—tacular! I'm spic—torious! I'm indi—spic—able!"

And I stared at him and stared at him till he couldn't take it no more, and me and Ivan rode our bicycles off into the sunset.

Later on that night, in our tent, me and Ivan figured out that since we were spics, then our whole families must be spic-sapiens mondongo-morphs, and that when we have picnics together it's a spic-nic. And we made a promise to each other that no matter where we went or what we did, our whole lives would be nothing less than a Spic-O-Rama! *(Lights down)*.

KRAZY WILLIE

(*When the lights come up, the headlights of the car pop on behind the chain-link fence and we hear banging coming from under the car. Krazy Willie slides from underneath the car on a dolly wearing his Desert Storm hat with the brim folded up off his face, dark Ray-Bans, a football jersey lifted over his head and worn across his shoulders, camouflage pants, and combat boots with his BVDs sticking out. He sports a Vandyke goatee and holds a can of beer in a brown paper bag. He looks up to a window across the street, beyond the audience.*)

KRAZY WILLIE: *(To his friend, Chewey, stage right:)* This is the shit!
Chew, this is the shit! *(Jumps on hood of car; radio comes on.)* It's over
for her, man, down by law. *(To window:)* Yo, yo, Yvonne. Krazy rules!
Yo, Yvonne, I dedicate this song to you, baby. *(Kicks car, starting
music.)* Krazy rules! Check this out.

(Sings to music:)

> She was black as the night
> Krazy was whiter than white

(To Chewey:) Yo, don't jump in, man, you throw me off. Shut the
fuck up! *(Sings to Yvonne again:)*

> Danger danger when you taste brown sugar
> Krazy fell in love overnight

Yo, yo, Yvonne. Yvonne, come on, baby! I'm giving you another
chance. How about it, baby? *(Pauses.)* What do you mean, why do we
both have to go? Because it's our fucking wedding, that's why!

Just shut up and listen! *(Sings:)*

> Nothing bad it was good
> Louie had the best that he could
> When he took her home to meet his momma and papa
> Louie knew just where he stood

*(Interrupted by voice from offstage hollering for him to shut up. Yells
back:)* Yo, am I singing to you? So mind your business! I'm singing

to my alleged bride. I've got your off-key right here, motherfucker. *(Pauses.)* Go 'head, call the cops. You can kiss my culo! *(Moons figure offstage and sings:)*

Louie Louie Louie Louieee

(Screams to onlooker:) Take a good look, motherfucker. *(Sings:)*

Louie Louie Louie Louaaa . . .
She was black as the night . . .

(Pulls up pants, signals Chewey to cut radio, and yells up at window again:) Yvonne, do you see the things I'm doin' for you, baby? Goddammit, I know you hear me. I see your shadow—I know that big ole coochie anywhere. All right, Yvonne, you're leaving me no choice. *(Pulls gun from pocket.)* I'll do it. I'll do myself in. *(Puts gun in mouth.)* I'll blow out my brains. *(Puts gun in crotch.)* All right, Yvonne, I'm gonna shoot the thing you love most. *(Pauses.)* Damn, is nothing sacred to you?! *(Jumps off car.)*

I can't believe that fuckin' shit! Shut up, Chew. It ain't over till I say it's over. I'll house her. I'mma school her. *(Climbs over fence.)* Yo, Yvonne, if I can't have you nobody can. I ain't goin' out like that. *(Aside:)* She thinks she's all that. *(To window:)* Yvonne, you think you're Miss Subway 1992, don't you? *(Goes for pay phone. Mumbles under breath:)* Heads will roll, butts will be kicked, faces will be slapped, feelings are gonna be hurt.

(On the pay phone:) What do you mean I gotta put a quarter in? I'm only calling across the street. I went to Desert Storm—you should

give it to me for nothing . . . Bitch! Reach out and touch this . . . *(Steps back, shoots phone, then puts gun in crotch by mistake.)* Damn, that shit is hot! *(Pours beer down pants to put out sting.)* Damn, that shit is cold!

(To Chewey:) Do I deserve this? Do I deserve this? I'm a hero, man. Why is she dogging me like that? All I did was say, "Look, look, baby, I'm just back from the greatest victory America has ever had and I need some time to get my head together. So let's explore the world around us—see other people, but just to test the strength of our relation . . . cha cha-cha cha-cha cha-cha."

All right, busted. What I was really thinking is: Fuck, I can score any nena I want cause I'm young, gifted, and Latino. Word, let me tell you. Yo, I know I'm not no Arnold Schwartz-a-nigger. You know, that's a name that happens to offend black people twice, you fugly puta-head.

Well, she's on my jock, playing hurt. *(Imitates Yvonne:)* "All you wanna do is skeeze. That's all you wanna do. Cause ever since you came back you got no money. You never take me out. You never buy me pretty things. You're twenty-nine years old and nowhere, hanging out with losers." She was talking about you, Chew. Why can't she just lower her standards? I did. She's forever telling me how sorry she is that Andy Garcia is married—like she had a shot!

But I persist and get my wish. Pero, ojo what you wish for, Chewey, porqué you might get it!

So, I steps. I go to the beach to reconnoiter and—may I tell you, little brother man? It is like paradise. Every type of mad girl is there—las morenitas, las negritas, hasta las feitas. And I'm rappin' at this one and I'm rappin' at that one. And the next thing I know, the sun has set and I have rapped to every single one of them and got—nada. Culo. Dick. Just mine, that's it.

So I fall back to Yvonne's crib on the double and I weasel her. Oh, I'm seriously weaselin' her. "Yo, yo, yo, baby. It's a miracle! This one day has been enough for me. I've pulled myself together." And she's all, "What are you doing here? I thought we were supposed to be testing the strength of our relationship." *(Sucks teeth.)* "Huh?" *(Sucks teeth.)* "Mister War Hero. Hmm? Hmm? Hmm?" *(Sucks teeth again.)* If she would of sucked her teeth one more time, Chew . . .

So what do I do? I have to retrench and go to the usual—begging. "Take me back, baby! I was a bobo, tú sabes. War heroes say and do stupid things sometimes. I was just going through a lot of pressure"—always blame it on pressure, Chew. When in doubt, psychologize—"So I'm going through a lot of pressure, but I'm feeling a lot better now. So why don't you suck my dick?" Na, I didn't say that! But it's the thought that counts!

But then I bust out with, "Yo, baby, let's get married. Cause, I'm going to take care of you like no man has ever taken care of a female. And as a bonus—as a bonus—I'mma let you have my babies."

But I don't see her respondin', verdad? And I'm getting suspicious. Cause she's looking way too happy for her. So I kick it to her real dead dead calm and nonchalant, you know me. "Did you meet anyone or anything happen for you today . . . cha cha-cha cha-cha. And she kicks it back just as frosty, "Oh, no, why?" Qué mentirosa. Quá embustera. I know she's lying to me, man. Cause my mother said to me, "Yo, mijo, women will lie to you. I'm the only woman who will tell you the truth." So I but play her right back. "Come on, baby, I'm not gonna get mad. It was my idea, right? So did you get lucky and shit? Cause if we can't be honest and trust each other what have we had, baby?"

Boom, she fesses that she's already had one smokin' date today and she has another coming up in a half hour to take her to the Palladium on Tropical Night. "And thank you so much for suggesting this, cause I'm finding out so much about myself that I did not know before. And now could you please leave?" Yo, I stop hearing her talk and all I see is her mouth moving and getting bigger and bigger and bigger. (*Mimes with hand.*)

And she's buggin', "Get out of my house! I knew you were gonna go crazy, Krazy. You're just like your father." And I say, "Well, you're just like my mother." And she says, "You're hopeless!" And I say, and I say . . . What did I say? *(Pauses, then shouts.)* "Fuck you!" Cause I couldn't think of nothing better to say.

P.S., next thing I know I'm walking all the way from the fucking projects to Jackson fucking Heights. And I'm thinking three things: a) She used me, b) I helped her use me, and 3) I wish her father had used a condom.

(Chewey makes to leave.) Come on, man, where you going? What's up with that? Come on, don't be a pussy. Stick with me. Yo, you got no place to go, Chew. You a loser too, puta-head.

(To Yvonne:) Go ahead, ho. You know what I'm going to do? I'mma give you to five, then I'm gonna kill you, bitch. One Mississippi. Two Mississippi. *(Pulls out gun.)* No, no, you know what I'mma do? I'mma go to the Palladium and do a Happy Land Two. That's what I'm gonna do. *(Kicks and smashes his head against the fence.)*

(To Chewey:) Chewey man, help me out! It hurts like coño. I can't live without her. If I were to make love to another woman right now I'd still be making love to Yvonne. Cause she's the only woman that didn't make me feel like a zero. That's why. And how am I going to go to my wedding womanless? My father's gonna give me so much beef—oh, my God, you don't know!

God, I miss the seventies. It was the best time of my life: Huggy Bear, angel dust, the Partridge Family . . . *(Breaks into song:)*

I was sleeping,
And right in the middle of a good dream,
Like all at once I wake up
From something that keeps knocking at my brain.
Before I go insane
I hold the pillow to my head
(Mumbles next two phrases:)
I think I love you!
I think I love you!

What do you mean, get another woman? If I could get another woman do you think I'd be out here suffering like this?! If I got another woman you know what that would do to Yvonne? Another woman would make her loca. Another woman would make her homicidal. Another woman would make her . . . appreciate my finer qualities!

Oh, my God, Chew, I'm a genius! I'm a fucking genius! I found my salvation. I need to borrow your woman. *(Pauses.)* Why you comin' outcha face like that? I'd do it for you.

Come on, Chew, friends don't let friends stay dissed. And may I remind you, Mister Ungrateful Ingrate, the time I went down to the draft board as your little fuckin' boyfriend to get you out: "If you want a chick with a dick call nine-seven-oh Kathy." And *I'm* the one who ended up going to Desert Storm. I risked my life, shot people who look like us but with towels on their heads, to protect your American way of life. And then when I ask you for one little fucking favor—one little fucking favor—this is what I get? You un-American fuck! I can't even look you in your face. Asqueroso. Porquería. Inútil. *(Pauses.)* That's a lot better.

Okay, okay. Your mission, dog-face Chew, is to authorize your female, Epiphany, to marry me at seventeen hundred hours. Then we'll rendezvous at Our Lady of Suspicious Miracles as schedulized. Cause as soon as I peeps Yvonne bustin' in through the church doors, I'mma skip the "I do's"! I'm gonna ram my tongue so far down Epiphany's throat that when I pull back babas gonna be drippin' off her chin. *(Closes eyes, vividly mimes simultaneous tongue insert and pelvis grind.)* And I'm gonna press her so close she's gonna *know* I'm not circumcised.

And she won't be able to take it no more. Right. *(Pauses. To Chewey:)* No, *Yvonne* won't be able take it no more. Epiphany's gonna be having a great time. *(Back to fantasy:)* And she'll let out a scream. One of those you can hear in Jersey. "No, baby, no! I'm sorry, baby. I do, I do." And I'll say, "You do?

You do? Well, baby, I . . . *don't!"* (*Pulls in fist in silent triumph.*)
Ouch!!! Hurtin', hurtin'. Just like she hurt me, la majadera.

Then, finally, I'll put her out of her misery . . . and marry her. And
I'll give Epiphany back to you. Better than ever. And I'll be large. I'll
be the flavor with my cinnamon goddess back on my arm where she
belongs. (*Sings:*)

> Metale semilla a la maraca pa que suene
> cha cu cha cucu cha cu cha

You know what time it is? Synchronize. Operation Recapture
Yvonne is in full effect. Attention! (*Pulls himself erect.*) Present arms!
(*Swigs beer.*) Forward . . . march! (*Sings:*)

> Your left, your left
> Your left, right, left.
> My back is aching, my belt's too tight,
> My cojónes are shaking from left to right.

Double time.

> Your left, your left,
> Your left, right, left.
> Frankenstein stole my wine
> That dirty motherfucker does it all the time . . . (*Marches offstage.*
> *Lights down.*)

RAFAEL

(A spotlight beams on, illuminating Raffi, standing stage right in front of a triptych of mirrors. He wears a blond wig, blue contacts, and a robe that only exposes his legs and black-socked feet.)

RAFAEL: *(To mirror:)* If you pricketh *(Stabs air with saber.)* a Latino doth he not bleedeth? If you tickleth a Latino doth he not giggleth? *(Breaks into a falsetto giggle, as if being tickled.)*

(Lights up. To audience:) Do you like my British accent? Do you think it's real? I'm not telling you. Do you like my albino looks? Do you think they're real? I'm not telling you that either.

I *will* tell you that I'm on the verge of a major breakdown—breakthrough—breakthrough in my heretofore minor career.

You see, I am an understudy at the not-for-profit production of *The Canterbury Tales.* Yes, yes, someone finally took ill so I'm going on

as the cuckolded innkeeper's manservant's best friend's friend's . . . friend. *(Spins around.)* Regarde . . . *(Recites with old English music playing:)*

> Whan that Aprill with his shoures sote,
> The droghte of Marche hath perced to the rote,
> And bathed every veyne in swich licour
> Of which vertu engendred is the flour.

(Snaps fingers and music turns off.) You got it? It's a *major* opportunity. Any actor in his right mind would kill for it. Besides, acting jobs are like sex: all around, but I don't seem to be getting any. You know what I mean?

(Walks to far side of bed and removes robe, revealing a black-and-white vertically-striped button-down shirt and black-and-white polka-dot boxer shorts. Pulls on a pair of black supertight stretch jeans.) But I'm not taking any chances this time. Oh, no! I'm wearing height enhancement shoes, to get that *lengthy* look. *(Displays black Frankenstein platform shoes with white stripes on the sides of the platforms, then puts them on.)* And I'm also going to be wearing this vertically striped shirt to get

that *lengthy* look. *(Displays shirt.)* And
I'm also going to be stuffing my shorts
*(Rapidly removes forty or fifty tissues from
box one at a time while speaking.)* to get
that . . . yes, that's right, that *lengthy*
look. *(Stuffs huge wad of tissues into
boxers, then buttons jeans around the
bulge, which sticks out the open fly.)*

*(Gazes at reflection in the mirror,
then down at his stuffed shorts.
Recites with Scottish accent:)*
"Is this a dagger which I see
before me? The handle
towards my . . . my . . . my . . ."
(To mirror:) Excuse me, squire, are
you that actor? Aren't you
that famous actor? *(To audience:)* Guilty as charged.

(Feigns shame.) All right, I confess. You were going to find out
anyway . . . *(To audience:)* Please
look me in the face! The rumors
are true. I am the love child of Sir
Laurence Olivier. Here's the true
untold story. Laurence—Larry—
met me mum in Puerto Rico while
shooting *The Boys
From Brazil*. Me mum was pressing his trousers . . .
(Mimes and sings:) "I want to live in America—" when Larry sneaks

up behind her in his undies *(Mimes.)*, grabs her bum, and whispers, "Ooh, I like young girls—their stories are shorter." Et voilà, mon frères! Je suis ici.

(To mirror:) Excuse me, aren't you that love child? Aren't you that famous bastard? *(To audience:)* Guilty as charged.

(Banging and muffled shouts from offstage. To bedroom door:) No, William, I'm not coming out. *(Pauses.)* I don't care! *(Pauses.)* No, I wouldn't attend your wedding if it was on *Star Search. (Pauses; rehearses sword fight.)* I don't have to come out and fight like a man. *(Elaborately flings cape over shoulders.)* I'm an actor, you gender-specific fascist. *(As he continues to talk, he puts a big jeweled cross on a gold chain around his neck. The look now resembles an Elizabethan costume.)* William, do you realize that you are a biological accident? Oh, yes, Mister Y-chromosome, why don't you go play with your little pre-woman? *(Imitating Willie badly:)* "Yo, Yvonne, let's get married, join the army, travel the world, meet interesting people and kill them." *(Aside:)* Yes, William, you're a hero . . . and so is a Blimpie.

(To audience:) I'm sorry. I'm very sorry. I must apologize for my brother. He's been on edge ever since Yvonne made a play for me. I'm not bragging, I'm sharing.

You see, I was working at Tele . . . Tele . . . How do you say it? Telemundo? I was dubbing movies at the time. You might remember me as the voice of Curly, in Spanish. *(Does impression of Curly:)* "Wooop. Pues claro. Un sinvergüenza, eh? Nyauh, nyauh! Pues yo debo."

Yvonne comes down to the studio to see what goes on behind the scenes. Well, no sooner are we alone than my slight hint of masculinity whips her into insensate desire, and being the occasional heterosexual that I am, I allowed her to have her way with me. But whilst our anatomies were coinciding, I could not stop thinking, "My life has no real purpose, no aim, no direction. I'm in complete self-denial, and yet I'm truly happy. I don't get it. What am I doing right?" And I looked down and I had lost the will. *(Addresses a male audience member:)* You know what I'm talking about? I knew you would. *(To all:)* So I faked an orgasm. I had never done this before in my life, but it's really quite simple: *(Mimes:)* I flipped her over on her front. I moaned and carried on—"Oh, oh"—pulled out, and spat on her back. I felt terrible. It was the first false note in an otherwise flawless performance.

(To mirror:) Are you that actor? Excuse me, squire, aren't you that famous actor? *(To audience:)* Guilty as charged!

Oh, God, I don't want to be with anyone whom I love more than myself. *(Inspects reflection.)* I'm not black. I'm not white. What am I? *(Sudden horror.)* I'm urine-colored, I'm actually urine-colored! *(Composes himself and adjusts wig. Shuts mirror triptych.)*

Well, I don't know why people insist on knowing themselves. It's hard enough to know what to wear. *(Crosses room to window.)* Oh, I don't care. I don't care. I'm not going to do anything I'm supposed to any more. I'm going home.

(Opens bedroom window and a Spanish Harlem-type cacophony invades room. Slams window shut. Silence.) It's so hard being Elizabethan in Jackson Heights. *(Walks toward television, next to mirror.)* But I don't care. I'm going to jet myself to London, nonetheless. I'll mingle with the palace pageantry. Have a fling with Di or Fergie. Perhaps Di *and* Fergie.

(A video of Laurence Olivier as the rabbi talking to Neil Diamond in The Jazz Singer *plays on a television above the mirror.)* Oh, look, it's me loving father, Laurence. *(To Laurence:)* Hello, Daddy. I'm coming to visit you.

LAURENCE: *(On screen.)* No!

RAFAEL: Yes, I'm going to live with you! *(Exits out the window.)*

LAURENCE: No!! I have no son!!!

RAFAEL: *(Peeks through window back at audience.)* You do now, ducky! *(Lights down.)*

JAVIER

(Stage dark. Dim spot follows Javier as he makes his way onstage in a wheelchair. His body is twisted beneath a very baggy gray sweat suit and white socks. He speaks slowly, with great effort, and occasionally drools.)

JAVIER: Okay, Miggy, turn the camera on. *(Brighter spot flicks on from wing. Sings:)*

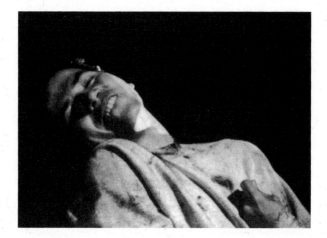

For he's a jolly good fella,
For he's a jolly good fella . . .

Willie, Willie . . . you're finally getting married. My condolences. You found a girl to stay with you. She must either be really ugly or really stupid. I wish you the best.

Mom, I'm sure you're looking as beautiful as ever. I'm sorry, I would of sent something sooner, but I probably spent it on a bottle or something. But, congratulations on the new little girl. Still overpopulating the planet, huh? We should just start that one-child policy the Chinese have; then we won't be starving to death, producing so much garbage.

Oh, yeah, pollution starts at home, Mom. Don't eat the tuna. The chicken's bad too, it's got salmonella. The beef has too much tetracycline. Vegetables have too many fucking pesticides. Can't drink the water—it has fluorocarbons. Can't breathe the air. Can't sit in the sun—no ozone. Can't sleep—noise pollution. TV rots our minds . . . Well, I'm fine, and I hope you're all doing well.

Hope I'm not disturbing this little dinner party. Just turn me off anytime. Like you always do.

(Bitter laugh.) I know right about now Dad's saying to himself, "Enough of this shit. There's Yolanda. How can I get her in the bathroom and do her?" Well, fuck your sex life, Dad! This is my moment. And I wanna talk about my sex life. See, we're really not so different, you and me. We both have somewhat of a sexual problem. And the problem is that we both want to have sex. But only one of us can. Where's the justice in that? Oh, I've tried everything. I'm exhausted.

I've explored all my fantasies and theirs. I've had women wear everything. I've tried every technique from the Kama-sutra to the Pink Pussy Cat.

I even went so far as to go to a sex therapist, but the access ramp only went to the second floor. So I got stuck with a dominatrix, Mistress Vanna Blanca, who stripped me naked, handcuffed me, wrestled me to the ground, then whipped my ass till it was raw.

She made me confess to things I never even knew existed. Ordered me to "suck and fuck and cook and clean. Now stop slobbering, you pig. And get on all fours and get banged like a bitch." And believe you me, Dad, I wanted to obey. But the only thing I wanna be good for I'm not even good at.

And this Vanna, well, I call her my girlfriend. She's the only one who ever loved me. And I can't please her, so I told her to get it wherever she can but not to fall in love. I don't know how long I can keep her like this. Tell me, Dad, how does it feel when you're inside them and you cum? Does the universe open up and for one moment you are made equal with the gods? You're a mambo king, an Aztec lord, an Inca prince. You're just every Hernandez and Fernandez! Isn't it wild, Dad? I'm telling you how it is!

You know, if this reincarnation thing is true, I'm definitely coming back as a blue whale. They're the largest species in the world. Can you imagine what an orgasm must be like for them? It must be huge.

If I could have an orgasm, then I could have a family, and if I could have a family I wouldn't fuck it up like you did. I know you're ashamed of me. But I'm more ashamed of you.

But don't worry about old Javier. I always get along without you somehow. I dance in my thoughts. I play basketball in my mind. And I get off in my dreams. See, Dad, everybody gets their *(Winces with headache pain.)* discount dream.

Do you ever think of all the people who have died? How many souls are out there trying to get into our bodies? Even mine. I think that's where we get headaches from. And I'm getting a headache right now, so I gotta go. Felicitaciónes, Willie, maybe I'll be there for Christmas. I don't know. Probably not.

(Shifts to leave, then thinks of one more thing.) Dad, remember that night when this gang was making fun of me outside the house: "Mira el mutant, mira el mutant." And you came out and you screamed, "What the hell are you doing to my son?" And you grabbed this guy's shirt so close he could taste your spit and you told him if you ever saw them on the block again you were going to kill each and every one of them . . .

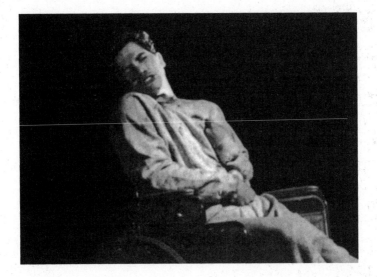

I fell in love with you that night, Dad. I couldn't believe you were the same man I had hated for all those years. Why can't you be that dad now?

Turn it off, Miggy! Vanna, get 'im out of here. *(Lights down.)*

GLADYZ

(Lights up. A funky seventies song plays. Gladyz is doing aerobics by the dryers while smoking a cigarette. She has a long, curly, hennaed mane of hair held back by a fuchsia headband, heavily mascaraed eyes, and bright red lips. She wears a fuchsia spandex off-the-shoulder top, fake Pucci spandex tights, a fantasy-gold necklace, big hoop earrings, a little gold watch, and spiked white pumps. In front of the row of dryers is a bench with a baby carriage nearby and a can of Diet Coke on the ground.)

GLADYZ: Work it . . . and work it . . . and work it . . . *(To Miggy, stage left:)* Go on, Miguelito, and play like a little gentleman. Mommy'll be right here doing her aerobics.

Miguelito, I said play nice. Don't rub soap in little Malaria's hair. Be a gentleman. And if you start to wheeze—sit down! No, not in the laundry basket, condenado. And use that inhaler, cause I don't want to spend my whole weekend in the hospital. What with Willie's wedding and all, I don't have the time, please.

(To Ofelia, downstage left:) I can't do this no more. No joda. All this just to be loved from the neck up.

(Picks handful of dirty laundry out of basket and inspects. To Miggy:) Miguelito, are these your brushstrokes? Mira, Ofelia, they're color-coded. Yellow in the front, brown for the back. *(Tosses clothes into machine, slams door.)*

(Coos to the baby in the carriage.) Ay, chichichita. Tan bonita la niña. Tan preciosa. *(To Ofelia:)* Ay, tenía que ser mia. *(To baby:)* Anisette. Tan cute. Anisette.

(Waves to Esperanza, downstage center:) Hola, nena! Esperanza—
bring your child-bearing hips over here. How you doing? Niña, you
look terrific. Let me tell you, twenty children haven't slowed you
down one bit. *(Pauses.)* I'm just teasing you. You look good. You
don't look chubby at all. You on a diet? I'm on a diet too, but what
you see is a very tall woman trapped in a very short body.

Ay, Espy, you shouldn't have. *(Takes package from Esperanza. Shouts:)*
Miguelito, Esperanza brought you some candy. *(Drinks from her Coke
can and addresses Esperanza:)* You shouldn't. *(To Miggy:)* Say thank
you. Always say thank you and please; that way you get more.

(To Esperanza:) Ay, mija, I can't stay and talk too long cause I'm going to lose my Krazy in a couple of hours. Sí, es sad, verdad. El primero, tú sabes. *(Whispers:)* It's not bad enough that that bruja Yolanda
bed my Felix. But now her Cubanoid little heifer of a daughter is
stealing my Willie.

(Back to Miggy:) Miguelito, don't interrupt me. Don't you see I'm
talking? Don't come to me with your problems. You don't see me

running to you every time I have a problem, do you? *(Pauses.)* Ay, Dios mío. Don't get loud with me. If she takes your bicycle just push her off!

(To girlfriends:) Ooops. I hope our most sacred lady of the hussies didn't hear me.

(Gladyz sees Miggy knock Malaria down.) Oopsie! *(Shouts:)* I'm sorry, Yolanda. I hope Malaria's okay. Miguelito, come over here right now! No joda zángano, lo cojo y lo vuelvo mierda. Le hago que le salgan plátanos por el culo. Come over here right now! I should slap you silly, cabróncito. *(Whispers confidentially to Miggy:)* I'm glad you knocked her down—just don't get caught next time. Go back and play like a little gentleman.

(Shouts:) I scolded him for you, Yolanda, now he's crying. I hope you're happy?

(To Esperanza:) Ay, mija, what did you do to your hair? What did you do to your hair? That is a do and a don't together. *(Snaps her fingers. Pauses.)* We marry beneath us—all redheads do. *(Pauses.)* No, this is not a hair weave. This is hair fusion. *(Puts cigarette on baby carriage.)* I could do that and more to my hair and Felix would not even notice. The romance has gone poof . . . limp. Tú sabes, like dead champagne. Ay, men today. *(Sighs.)* Ay. Ay. Ay. *(Baby coughs.)* Ay—Anisette! *(To Esperanza:)* She's trying to smoke. *(To baby:)* Ay, tan cute. Anisette, stop it. *(Pulls cigarette out of carriage and takes a big drag.)*

(To girlfriends:) Ay—look over there at that gorgeous papi! No, don't look. Now—look! No, don't look. Now. Isn't he gorgeous? He comes and does his jeans every day. The same jeans.

Ay, qué precioso. Isn't he ouch-looking? How do I look, nenas? Do I look okay? *(Pauses.)* Well, do I at least look good for me?

(She stands and strikes a seductive pose, then beckons to man.) Psst! Ksss. Ishmael. Ishmaelito. Yoo-hoo! *(To the girls:)* Isn't he ouch-looking? No invente papito. Me tiene—uutthh. *(Bites her hand.)* Ishmael . . . Ishmaelito . . . Ishy . . .

(To girlfriends:) Why is he talking to that buttless, anorexic third-world desgraciada!

I can't believe it. That witch musta put a spell on him. Well, looka-her, do you see the way she dresses? Do you see the way she moves? It's obscene. It's disgusting. It's perverse. Oh, God, I wish I were her!

(Sniffs the air.) Ay fo, qué's eso? Is that you? What's that smell? Somebody's insides are rotten. Ay, please—it's the baby. Anisette. No joda. Somebody please change her for me! *(Pushes carriage away. It rolls down the aisle of machines toward backstage.)* Ay, Dios mío, it never stops. All this responsibility. All day it's clean this, wipe that, take care of this. No wonder animals eat their young. You know, it's only a matter of time before she'll turn on me. Mija, let me tell you—it's a mother's curse. You hate your mother until you become one and then you are filled with the deepest respect. *(Sighs and throws down cigarette butt.)*

I never had a chance to be independent. All my life, somebody's always been on my tit. That's why they're hanging so low. Cause people don't like their women strong. Especially Spanish women—forget about it! We're just ornaments . . . female eunuchs. We're just allowed to nurture and understand, but God forbid we should go for what we want, cause then you're a bitch.

Ofelia, you're lucky you can't have children. Cause you're free to do . . . to do . . . What is it that you do? Well, whatever it is that you do. Ever since I was seventeen I've been raising four—five—five children. *(Retrieves baby carriage.)* You know what that's like? One of these afternoons . . .

(Spies Miggy climbing on machines.) Miguelito, if you fall off of that dryer and break your legs, don't come running to me.

(Takes a piece of chocolate cake from carriage. Eats while she speaks.) I wish I could change my name to Christmas or Electricity. Gladyz is so plain. Then everybody'd find me mysterious and I'd get invited to all the parties. I always wanted to have a life, one that I could talk about. Cause I had the brains but not the clothes—that's why I dropped out of high school.

Nenas, you know what I would like to do? You know what I'd like to do? I'd like to drink a pitcher of Yago Sant'Gria, rip off all my clothes, and run naked in the streets and hug all the ugly women and tell them that it's okay. There, I said it! I said it!

(To baby, who is fussing.) Ay. Qué te pasa, nenita? Chichichita, Anisette. She's having a bad dream. Shhh. Sana que sana, culito de rana. *(Pours Diet Coke into baby bottle. To Ofelia)* Don't worry, it's diet. Suck it up. There you go. Qué linda. Tan cute.

You know, if I do only one thing right it's to make sure her life is nothing like mine. *(Lights another cigarette.)* Did I tell you? I had a bad dream last night myself. I dreamt my mother had died. And I woke up sweating and crying, tú sabes. And I went running into her room and I hugged and kissed her and told her how I loved her. And she slapped me right in the face—for waking her up. It's the story of my life. She never forgave me for putting her in a home, and I'll never forgive myself for taking her out.

All day long it's "Ay, mija, I'm gonna die. Ay, mija, I'm gonna die."
I'm starting to like the sound of it. Oh, I know I'm the dark meat in
my family . . . And speaking of dark meat. *(Extracts a chicken leg from
carriage and munches delicately. Smokes, munches, smokes, munches.)*
Smoked chicken. Did you hear about her buttlessness and somebody's husband? Aha, aha, mmmmm. May God strike me down.
Que Dios me haga más vieja antes de mi tiempo if I'm lying to you.
Yes, I heard it from a very reliable source. Someone said to someone
who then told somebody else, then that somebody told me quite by
accident, so I know it's true. No, not Rosi's. No, not Mirtha's. *(Tosses
chicken leg into carriage.)* Did I say Agnes? *(Pauses.)* Yesss, it was
Cookie. It was Cookie. Imaginate! And they're supposed to be best
friends. See, mija, you can't trust other women, cause they'll say one
thing to your front and another to your behind.

Mira, Esperanza, if I was two-faced do you think I'd be wearing this
one? Por favor. Dios mío.

I'm not imagining things, Ofelia. She's trying to steal my Felix.
Once upon a lie he vowed to be my one and only, but now . . . *(To
customer:)* Excuse me, I'm talking! I'm sorry, Miss Lady, you can't get
your money back. You take your chances in this laundromat. Jodona
pendeja.

(Back to Esperanza:) Oh, he's out there wenching, mujeriando. One
day they'll find I killed my husband and I'm gonna plead voluntary
insanity.

(To another customer:) I'm sorry, Mister Man, I'm sorry. You got the
Vegas machine—you gotta keep putting quarters in till one of them
hits.

(To the ladies:) I'm thinking of letting Felix come back to the house. *(Pauses.)* Yes, but on probation. Cause as bad as he is, he's one of the better ones. It's a recession everywhere. Anyway, she's only this year's model. And if I catch him again—that's it. I'm taking the house and my boys and I'm going to make them the best little men of Jackson Heights.

(Sees Miggy pummeling another child.) Miguelito, papá, don't hit anybody unless they are down.

Ay, coño bendito, I didn't realize what time it was. I have to take the F train to el culo de New York. Miguelito, let's go.

(To the girls, as she collects her belongings:) Well, it's been muy fun. Bien nice y chévere. Chaito. Ofelia, could you close for me? And don't give any money back—it's the American way.

(Calls to Miggy:) Miguelito, come on, we're going to be late for the wedding. *(Pauses.)* Well, push her off if it's your bike. What are you, a boy or girl? Knock her down. That's it. See you, nenas. So long, Yolanda. See you at the wedding. If you can scrape yourself off the floor, you nasty bitch!!!! *(Pushes carriage offstage. Lights down.)*

FELIX

FELIX: *(Offstage to Yolanda:)* That's very Spanish of you. It's gonna take more than a little spritz to put out my fire, baby.

(Felix walks onto center stage, where there is a spotlight. He is a middle-aged, corpulent man with graying hair and a thick black mustache. He wears a black tuxedo with a white carnation on the lapel and black patent leather shoes. He is holding a mike in one hand and a glass of champagne in the other. Visibly drunk, damp, and disheveled, he mops his face with a handkerchief.) Epa! Epa! Qué rico! Sabrosito! Menealo!

Well, here we are at Grand Prospect Hall, where all your dreams come true. It's not the Magic Kingdom, but if you close your eyes, it's only a hop and a skip. We gotta push things along, cause the Herkowitz funeral is next. Grandma, you can stay.

Okay, I'm gonna sing a song. *(To band:)* Okay, knock it off. Let's give it up for the band. *(Applauds.)* You boys played real good. Thanks,

boys. I'm gonna give you a big tip: Don't fry bacon in the nude. *(Drum and cymbal—ba dump ba.)* I'm gonna sing a song, cause my father sang at my wedding. And I've selected a special tune for this occasion. Cause everybody thinks Colombians are in the Mafia, so we might as well take advantage of it. It goes something like this: *(Sings:)*

> Speak softly love and hold me warm against your heart
> The trembling vows we made will live until we die
> I told the truth Then lied some more
> Porqué tú me haz jodido y no puedo más
> Y no es mi culpa I said mm-hmm
> She probably said mm-hmm *(Hums a line, then whistles.)*

It's too painful. It brings back too many memories of my father and of Gladyz when she was young and beautiful.

Ah, life! Tell me, isn't it moments like this that make you think about the meaning of life? I've been thinking a lot about it lately. Even the great philosophers have wrestled with this one and come up empty. What is life? Anybody! *(Sighs.)* What the fuck difference does it make? The first half is ruined by your parents and the second half destroyed by your kids. That's life!

Now, I know the newlyweds would be disappointed if I did not speak at length about matrimonio. So listen up, amigos y socios, Yvonne. Willie, as I told you from the time you were yo high, and I can never tell you enough: Lies, distortions, half-truths, and critical omissions are the glue to all relationships.

Uncle Brother, stop drinking like it's the end of the world. *(Pauses.)* No, it's not the blood of Christ. It's sangría. *(Pauses.)* Oh, go ahead and put a curse on me. I already live in New York—what more can you do to me.

(To newlyweds:) So I'm going to teach you two how to keep that matrimonio fresh and alive, when what you really wanna do sometimes is put a bullet through your head. Fantasize. Fantasize. There is absolutely nothing wrong with taking the body of a woman you desire and superimposing it over the tired old thing at home.

What else? What else? You're also gonna fight a lot, which is really a lucky thing cause sex is never as good as after a vicious fight . . . right, Gladyz? My little gladiatress. Nothing like rough sex! *(Barks.)*

When I was younger I used to have . . . what do they call that now? Anybody! Performance anxiety. Now I just look forward to giving it my best shot and coming out of it alive. Many a night I have come home to Gladyz and asked her for a little cabeza and she says, "I'm too tired, I'm too tired." And I tell her, "Baby, it'll be over before you know it. You won't feel a thing."

If I was a young puppy again, instead of the old dog that I am! Yvonne, yum, Yvonne, you look nice. There're so many things I could've done to your Bosco candy-coated thighs.

(*To Willie who has shouted at Felix:*) Hey, Willie, what are you getting so upset about? Oh, all of a sudden you're man enough to take me on? (*Takes off jacket.*) I never raised my hand to my father, cause if I had (*Begins sparring.*) I wouldn't be here to punch you into place. Et tu, Raffi? Et tu? Go ahead, both of youse. You get the first punch, then I get a shot.

Back off, Gladyz, back off! What are you taking their side for? It's my money that paid for this hall. It's my hall, it's my liquor, it's my cake, and I'll do whatever the fuck I please. You wanna hit me too? (*Rolls up sleeves.*) So everybody here wants to take a shot at me. Come on, I'll take everybody on. Everybody except you, Ofelia. I never fight with ugly people . . . they got nothing to lose.

I'm not drunk. Never been more sober in my life. *(Pauses.)* No, baby, I've had to eat it for so long I've had it up to here. What this family needs es una enema grandisima! *(Nasty gesture.)*

Shut up, I'm getting to the toast. Here's to Krazy Willie. What kind of name is that for a grown man, huh? To my firstborn. I love you, but you're a disappointment. I'm sorry, but you're a big disappointment. I couldn't make you a man. The war couldn't make you a man. What makes you think in your wildest dreams that this poor sixteen-year-old titty-bopper's got a shot? Don't run away from me. Everybody, look at the pussy go. *(To Yvonne:)* Don't worry, sweetheart, he always comes crawling back.

And here's to Raffi: to my son, who is an extra in his own family. I love you . . . in my own way. But you're a liar. You're a goddamn liar. Why do you refuse to acknowledge me as your father? Answer me! Answer me! Did I beat you? Did I abuse you? Maybe, maybe—but you have to be resilient in life.

Where's my favorite little nerd? Where is he? Miguelito, come over here. Come here, papá. Come over here. What are you so afraid of? Go ahead, keep following in Willie's footsteps and one day he's gonna stop short and you're gonna find your head going right up his ass. But I love you cause I know you're mine. I had a blood test done.

(To a wedding guest:) Eh, what are you whispering over there? Why don't you say it to my face? Let me tell you something. There's nothing Felix Leopardo Gigante hasn't heard already. A toast to myself: What can be said about me? That I tried to be more and better. That I tried not to make the same stupid mistakes my father made.

At least I was there for youse. I gave up a lot to provide for youse.

I never told you this but I had a shot to travel with Carlos Santana. That's right—Mister Oye Cómo Va. He came up to me personally and said that I was the best maracas player he'd ever heard. Then Gladyz got pregnant with Willie, then wichoo, Raffi, and then Javier . . . *(Lowers head, overtaken by emotion.)* Oh, my God, Javier. And it destroyed my chance. Cause I could of played with one of the great Latin rock and rollers. Grabbed God by the ears and kissed him right smack on the lips. But I chose to stick it out and give you what

I could, and what do I got? My memories. Youse . . . *(Pauses and reflects a moment.)*

I have a confession to make. Unbeknownst to Gladyz here, I had an affair once. I'm sorry, baby. I admit it. But it kept me from running away and it helped me to understand you. *(Pats gut.)* Kept me young. It's not that we men want more sex than women, it's that we want a different kind of sex. More often. Right, fellas? *(Silence.)* Well, don't all back me up at once. *(To Gladyz:)* Ever since you had the kids, you only want it when Jupiter aligns with Mars.

I ask myself, where would I be without you by my side? Pushing me, kicking me, nailing me to the wall. Cause deep in my heart, I believe that any woman can make love to a handsome man, but it takes a great woman to keep making love to an ugly pig like me. To my gordita.

Go, get out of here, go to him, Yvonne. You have my blessing. Enjoy your honeymoon. Why he's taking you back to the gulf, I don't know. But promise me, Yvonne, my new daughter, that you'll always be there to fix it, mend it, make it better, and if it doesn't work out then, remember, you always have family. And tell my son that no matter how much he hates me, I'll always be here for him, cause we're stuck with each other.

Now I want the rest of you to hurry up and enjoy the festivities. I gotta take a leak. *(Picks up jacket, trails offstage as lights go down.)*

(Lights up. Miggy comes into his bedroom, dragging his feet. He is ready for bed, wearing his stocking cap, teeth with overbite, thick glasses, over-sized blue-and-white flannel pajamas, and two different-colored tube socks dangling from his feet. He speaks in a low, sad voice.)

MIGGY: I lost my hero, Krazy. I lost my hero, Krazy. *(Mopes, then suddenly cheers.)* But I got all his stuff! *(Goes to his box.)*

(Playacts. As emcee:) Miggy, welcome to "Yo MTV Raps." We hear you're a great dancer.

(As himself:) Well, you can't believe everything you hears.

(As emcee, fake humble:) You've been selected out of millions of kids for this dance competition.

(As wildly enthusiatic self:) Okay, I'm a Sagittarius. I love chocolate ice cream.

(As emcee:) Go! *(Hits music.)*

(Dances, as himself.) Did I win yet? Did I win yet? I won! I won! What do I win?

(As emcee:) You win your own Nintendo Super Mario Brothers and a lifetime pass to Club MTV.

(As himself:) I won! I won! I'd like to thank all the little people who I had to step on to make it here. *(Gasping and wheezing, fishes inhaler from breast pocket and inhales a squirt.)*

(Anxious pause. To mother behind bedroom door.) Noise? What noise? I'm not doin' nothing. I'm just resting. *(Pauses.)* Yes, yes, yes. I'm already studying that old ridiculous encyclopedia—so there! You tell me things a million trillion zillion times that I forget cause you tell me so many times. *(Pauses.)* Na-ha. I'm not gonna go to sleep, cause that stupid old wedding took up my valuable time. *(Throws tantrum.)* Now I know why people get married. It's so they can have children and make somebody else's life miserable.

(Jumps from bed to chin-up bar and hangs.) I want to be a basketball player. I want to be a basketball player. God, please don't make me a jockey. Am I Michael Jordan yet?

No *(Lets go of bar, falls to bed)*, because my parents made me genetically deficient in height chromosomes. They must be punished.

(Leaps off of bed and establishes a mock court at the foot. As himself:) I herebywith take Mister and Missus Gigante to court.

(As counselor:) Your Honor, my client has suffered because of abuse and negligence.

(As himself:) Yes. I can't even take care of myself, so why do I have to take care of my useless sister and vacuum the dog? I'm a child, not a slave. And I don't want to go to the Fresh-Air Fund with some family I don't even know, like a hostage. They could be murderers and have bones and skulls of other Fresh-Air Fund victims in the refrigerator. *(Screams.)*

(As parents:) But Your Honor, we have done all we can. He just doesn't deserve anything. He won't finish his encyclopedias. He doesn't eat his vegetable goo . . .

(As himself:) Objection, time out, illegal!

(As parents:) But Your Honor, we're doing everything—

(As judge:) Shut up!

(As parents:) But why?

(As judge:) Because it's the law. Go on, my son.

(As himself:) Thank you, Your Honor. They argue in Spanish so we won't understand what they are saying. But we speak Spanish too!

(As judge, to Miggy:) I herebywith give you custody of yourself to yourself.

(To parents:) And you must wear your dirty underwears on your heads. Recess.

(As himself to mother behind bedroom door again:) I can't hear you, Mom. I'm a giant Ninja Turtle taco. *(Crawls under quilt that has Mutant Ninja Turtles all over it.)* Na-ah. I'm not gonna take that nasty medicine. Why don't you take it? *(Pauses.)* I didn't say nothing. I said thank you for reminding me, Mommy dearest. *(Pauses.)* Okay, don't take me to the hospital. I'm gonna report you to the ASPCA for child abuse.

(Hanging upside down over the edge of the bed. His head touches the ground. Muses to himself:) What if I killed myself? Then they'd be sorry. Here lies the most good boy Miggy who never got what he deserved. I'll say *yes* to drugs. *(Flings off quilt and shouts:)* Yes. Yes. Yes. Yes. Yesss!!

(To door:) Okay, shut up. I'm already goin' to sleep. *(To himself:)* God, I hate this house. I hate this family. I hate this asthma. I wish I were dead. I don't mean that, God. It's just for them. Okay?

(To door:) Mom? Mom? You know, Mom, it won't be long before I'm all grown up and one day you're gonna wake up and ask yourself, "Where did all the time go? Miggy is so big and I never let him have any fun. That must be why he never visits me anymore." And you'll have nasty elephant ankles and you'll drool and be deaf and lonely in a home. And they won't let you play either.

(Sound of parents fighting offstage filters through the door.)

(Sings with eyes closed and fingers in ears:)

Miggy's in the house, y'all
I said 'M' to the 'I' to the 'G' to the 'G'
to the
'Y,' y'all
I'm a hip-hop junkie . . .

I know what I'll do! I'll make my molecules vibrate so fast I'll be invisible and I'll run away, travel the world from galaxy to galaxy at warp speed, and . . . *(Jumps and grabs chin-up bar. Looks upward.)* God, if you make them stop, I'll be the best little boy in the whole world. *(Muffled shouts continue.)* Okay, God, I'm warning you! If you don't make them stop, I'm never gonna believe in you. Okay, you asked for it, I'mma take the Virgin Mary and tie her up, put her in a brown paper bag, and if you ever wanna see your mother again, you'll do what I tell you.

(Bar retracts, lifting Miggy heavenward.) I didn't say nothing, mean-head. *(Lights down.)*

MAMBO MOUTH

A SAVAGE COMEDY

JOHN LEGUIZAMO

This text of *Mambo Mouth* is based on the original one-man show performed by John Leguizamo. *Mambo Mouth* was first produced, but not in its entirety, at the H.O.M.E. for Contemporary Theatre and Art on October 26, 1990, then mounted at The American Place Theatre's Sub-Plot Theatre on November 8, 1990. It moved to the Main Stage at the American Place on February 15, 1991. It moved again and for the last time to the Orpheum on June 2, 1991, and closed August 25, 1991.

H.O.M.E. for Contemporary Theatre and Art
DIRECTOR—Peter Askin
COSTUME CHANGES—Theresa Tetley

American Place Sub-Plot
DIRECTOR—Peter Askin
LIGHTING DESIGN—Graeme F. McDonnell
STAGE MANAGER—Joseph A. Onorato

SILHOUETTE—Theresa Tetley

SOUND DESIGN—Bruce Elman

SET DESIGN—Greg Erbach

American Place Main Stage

DIRECTOR—Peter Askin

SET DESIGN—Philipp Jung

SOUND DESIGN—Bruce Elman

MUSIC SUPERVISOR—JellyBean Benitez

COSTUME QUICK CHANGE—Theresa Tetley

PRODUCER—Wynn Handman

STAGE MANAGER—Michael Robin

Orpheum

PRODUCER—Island Visual Arts

LIGHTING DESIGN—Natasha Katz

SET DESIGN—Philipp Jung

STAGE MANAGER—Joseph A. Onorato

SILHOUETTE—Theresa Tetley

MUSIC SUPERVISOR—JellyBean Benitez

SOUND DESIGN—Bruce Elman

This book is for all the Latino people who have had a hard time holding on to a dream and just made do.

I met John Leguizamo on a Wednesday afternoon when I was auditioning twelve prospective students for my acting class. He performed a monologue from a war movie, and my inner Geiger counter immediately told me: "This is an extraordinary acting talent." I accepted him in my class with the expectancy of assigning a scene and a partner to begin the usual process of training. But he surprised me by bringing in a piece he had written. He was inspired by *Drinking in America*, a collection of dramatic monologues I had directed that was written and performed by Eric Bogosian at The American Place Theatre. John's character was a young man trying to get back in his girlfriend's good graces after she had locked him out of her house. While amusing and well acted, the situation and character were too limited to warrant further development; I suggested that he create another character. He later said, "I was encouraged, I made the old guy laugh."

He continually astonished the class and me with the vivid life he gave to an assortment of Latino characters who were ironic, multi-

dimensional, and daring. My studio became populated with a trans-
vestite, an illegal alien, a hardworking parent, a talk show host, and
others . . . each a full rendition with sound, props, complete costume.
Most important, each was honestly felt and accurately observed, coming from a deep organic source and always informed by an incredibly
high intelligence.

John felt the freedom to share the characters with the class in
early rough-draft versions—sometimes too long, sometimes not yet
fully developed or shaped. Through a process involving improvising
and directorial notes, the characters were brought to fuller realization. The laughter triggered by that first piece eventually turned into
cheers and strong applause from my class. This was more than en-
couragement from his peers; it was deep admiration. We had seen
the maturing of a really first-rate talent.

John has determination equal to all his other attributes, and he
soon, quite logically, found places to try out his characters around
New York. The favorable reception was no surprise. We had room
at The American Place Theatre to do the piece on a series of week-
ends in our small Sub-Plot Theatre. I suggested that Peter Askin, one
of my directing students, get to know John and his work. Peter was
enthusiastic, and the relationship seemed promising, so we moved
ahead. Their collaboration eventually took the shape of *Mambo
Mouth*, which opened on November 8, 1990. The demand for tickets
was so great that on February 15, 1991 we moved the show to our
large theatre. What began as classroom exercises blossomed into a
full-fledged off-Broadway hit.

WYNN HANDMAN

Wynn Handman is both a distinguished acting teacher and director
of the American Place Theatre in New York City which he cofounded

in 1963. His role in the theater since then has been to seek out, encourage, train, and present new, exciting writing and acting talent. At The American Place Theatre, several hundred productions of new plays by living American playwrights have advanced theater culture and have been reproduced at other theaters and on television and film. Always devoted to development, The American Place Theatre has produced the early work of many important contemporary playwrights, covering a broad spectrum of styles and ethnic origins.

Since the time he taught at The Neighborhood Playhouse School of the Theatre in New York, Wynn Handman has made an important contribution to the training of actors. In more than forty years of teaching, he has trained many outstanding actors, including James Caan, Michael Douglas, Sandy Duncan, Mia Farrow, Richard Gere, Cliff Gorman, Joel Grey, Raul Julia, Margot Kidder, Frank Langella, Burt Reynolds, Tony Roberts, Christopher Walken, Denzel Washington, and Joanne Woodward, as well as hundreds of others appearing in all media. Wynn Handman has also taught at the Yale School of Drama and is the editor of *Modern American Scenes for Student Actors.*

The first thing one notices after a few days' work with John Leguizamo, aside from his obvious gifts as an actor, is that he never stops writing. For a director and collaborator this is both blessing and curse. It is a luxury to have ample material to choose from, especially when it is usually strong stuff, funny, touching, raw, unexpectedly poetic—but when it never stops, slipping under your door at three AM, burying your desk, invading your personal life, your dreams, accompanying you on your honeymoon . . . well, we all have to make sacrifices for our art. Or our John.

Our collaboration began in June 1990, when Wynn Handman invited me to workshop *Mambo Mouth* with John in preparation for its November production at The American Place Theatre. Sitting in an audience of mostly family and friends well acquainted with his work (a developmental technique that John relies on), I watched a run-through of the monologues, some of which, like "Loco Louie," "Pepe," and "Manny the Fanny," were already substantially developed.

Other characters performed that night were subsequently dropped or incorporated into other monologues.

Even at that early stage, John enhanced his performance with costumes as well as the use of slides for "Crossover King." It is evident, I think, to anyone familiar with his work, that John could have performed *Mambo Mouth* in a T-shirt and jeans with wonderful results, and some felt that the elaborate costumes would detract from John's acting virtuosity. As for the comedic effect of the slides, one had only to be in the American Place audience the night the slide projector bulb burned out and witness John describe twelve *imaginary* slides with side-splitting results to know that the slide show, like the costumes, was only an option, not a necessity.

The summer was devoted to working on the text of *Mambo Mouth*, with September reserved for rehearsal of the play for a production at H.O.M.E., a small SoHo theater, the first week of October. Collaboration on the text went something like this:

MONDAY: We work on incorporating our favorite sections of an early monologue, "Tito Testosterones," into "Agamemnon" because of their similarities. John adds two jokes to "Loco Louie," three to "Manny the Fanny," and we review slides for "Crossover King." They are all used for comic effect and we have a great time laughing at them. Later, I realize that some of them are pictures of John's family. I make a note to watch my back.

TUESDAY: John arrives with new drafts of both "Tito" and "Agamemnon," four new jokes for "Loco," a totally new (at least to me) monologue about a bouncer, and we laugh at more slides for "Crossover King." He asks if I am photogenic.

WEDNESDAY: The monologue about the bouncer has now insinuated its way into "Angel," and along with six new jokes for "Loco" comes yet another new monologue about an Astor Place drifter selling dreams. This evolved into "Inca Prince," *Mambo Mouth*'s prodigal child, because it always promised more than it delivered. Its theme, the relationship between a failed father and his shamed son, was of particular interest to us both, only increasing our frustration that we could not get it right. Although "Inca Prince" was performed most of the time on stage, it was cut from HBO's presentation.

THURSDAY: John is filming *Hangin' with the Homeboys*, giving me time to concentrate on the same material two days running. There is a God!

FRIDAY: John returns with more new material. Where did he find the time? I am giddy with the news that John habitually writes until four A.M. If there is a God, She's at John's place, swapping material.

Variations of this schedule continued all summer. As September approached, deadlines to freeze the text were made and broken, then made again. I was learning that John's theatrical trunk held a world of characters, stories, and jokes developed over years of stand-up and improvisational work, and he *never* discarded material, especially if it had ever gotten a laugh.

And though the stories might change, it seemed as if he had known the characters like family for years. He could inhabit them at will, never concerned with making them likable, only truthful, instinctively aware that empathy, not sympathy, is the ultimate test of a character's universality.

John makes strong, often extreme choices in his writing as well as his acting, and rehearsals continued to explore the text, forcing the braggadocio of Agamemnon, Angel, and Loco Louie to the moment when a sudden glimpse of vulnerability stripped them bare. Agamemnon reduced to a Cuban cabana boy sweeping the sand; Angel finally forced to turn to his mother for help in front of the cops, and being refused; Loco Louie, unable to admit that his first sexual experience left him with questions not answers; Manny, the girlfriend from hell, taking charge of her life with the help of some Krazy Glue; Pepe, the illegal alien, giving voice to the silent minority of American citizens who are treated worse than illegal aliens; and the Crossover King, preaching the gospel of living a lie and at the same time hilariously incapable of following his own advice.

The October workshop at H.O.M.E. provided more opportunities to tighten the material, locate the unseen characters, find opportunities to interact with the audience ("Agamemnon," "Manny the Fanny," and "Crossover King"), experiment with the order of the monologues, and sharpen the costume changes. This last was critical to the pace of the show, and by the time *Mambo Mouth* reached the American Place, John and Theresa Tetley, his expert costume-changer, had the complicated changes down to a minute. The backstage intervals were initially accompanied by music, which was from the outset an important element of *Mambo Mouth*. Most characters entered and exited to music, and some (Agamemnon, Loco Louie, and Manny) danced as well as sang. To further tighten the interludes, we experimented with beginning the monologues backstage while John changed costumes. That idea was expanded to include a character continuing his monologue after his exit. Music, sound effects, dialogue, naked body parts, the backstage circus life of *Mambo Mouth*, became far too interesting to hide. With the American Place production, John began changing behind a scrim, and with Theresa exuberantly playing a number of roles (the cop who wallops Angel, Inca Prince's bickering wife, the maître d' who throws Manny out of the restaurant), their silhouettes extended the onstage life of one monologue even as John prepared for another. By moving closer or farther away from the scrim as well as adding lights and rear-projected slides, the audience was invited to imagine a world of *Mambo Mouth* that extended beyond the stage.

Mambo Mouth played for over nine months on four different stages, and during the entire run John continued to tinker with his writing and performance. When new material didn't fit existing characters, new characters began to form. The Gigante family, featured in *Spic-O-Rama*, began popping up in performance spaces downtown. Trusted family and friends, all astute directors and critics of John's work, began the developmental process again. Happily, so did I.

PETER ASKIN

Peter Askin most recently directed *Spic-O-Rama* for broadcast on Home Box Office, and onstage both in New York and at the Goodman Theatre in Chicago. Off-Broadway credits include *Mambo Mouth, Reality Ranch, Beauty Marks, Ourselves Alone, Reno,* and the New York and Los Angeles premiers of *Down an Alley Filled with Cats*. He has written for film (*Smithereens, Old Scores, Seasons Greetings, Selling Kate*), television (WNET's *Bet One I Make It*), and print (*The New York Times* and *Life* magazine). He has collaborated with John Leguizamo on a television comedy special and a new screenplay, *White Chocolate*. Peter Askin is married to actress/playwright Kim Merrill, and is the director of the Westside Theatre in New York City.

I was born in Latin America. I had to—my mother was there. But I came of age in the land that time forgot: Jackson Heights, Queens, the truest melting pot of New York City. It's a modern-day Ellis Island. All the peoples of the world stop there before they go on to wherever it is they have to go—Irish, Italians, Jews, Puerto Ricans, Dominicans, Chinese, Greeks, Colombians, Ecuadorians, and every possible combination thereof.

My upbringing is probably most remarkable for its transitions, and in many ways change has been the leitmotiv of my life ever since. We were constantly moving, so I went to a different school every year. Every year I had to make new friends and get used to new faces, new bullies, new girls, and new teachers. I lived in Bogotá, Colombia, till I was five; then Jackson Heights, Elmhurst, east Elmhurst, Astoria, and Jamaica, Queens; Manhattan's East Village, West Village, uptown, downtown, and midtown. Pick any of the many armpits of New York, and I've lived there.

My parents kept moving, but I found them. They were trying to

Jones-up, to fulfill the immigrants' dream of improving their life-
style. We started in a studio apartment with a Murphy bed, which
seemed like sci-fi from my third-world point of view. We then moved
to a one-bedroom apartment, then to a first-floor apartment with a
backyard, and finally to our own house. Unfortunately, all the rooms
but one were rented out, so we had to live as if we were in a studio
again.

I have one brother, on whom I inflicted all sorts of torture. I was
a mad Frankenstein and he was my monster. I often made him taste
things no human being has ever tasted—or ever will. How many
times did I pull his bathing suit down at Astoria Pool? How many
times did I try to smother him under a pillow just to get something
happening on a dull Sunday? Too often! Luckily for me, I was the el-
der brother, so there was no one to torture me—except my father.

When I say my father was a strict autocratic-totalitarian-despotic-
dictator-disciplinarian, I don't mean that in a negative way. He was in
love with culture, the word *culture*. He wanted everything to smack
of taste and decency, so he smacked culture into my brother and beat
the fear of God into me. He did this to show the world we weren't just
any immigrant Hispanic family just off the boat. His boys knew Puc-
cini and Matisse; we were classy.

In his youth my father studied film. When he was nineteen he fell
in love with Italian neo-realism and decided he wanted to be a director.
So he studied for two years at Cinecittà, one of the great filmmaking
studios in Italy. Family lore has it he mind-melded with Fellini while
both imbibed at the local trattoria. He returned to Bogotá when he was
twenty-one and immediately started a family. Having to bring home
the Kraft macaroni and cheese put an end to my father's cinematic
aspirations, but you could say I'm continuing the family tradition.

My mom is a very attractive and exotic (euphemism for ethnic-
looking) woman. She's part Native American, part Arab, part Spaniard,

and rumors pervade of Jewish and African contributions as well. She could have had any man in greater Bogotá, but chose my dad because he had that cosmopolitan Euro flair.

Growing up in Queens was a great education in comedy and survival. Unlike the other boroughs, gangs in Queens did not force you to participate; membership was voluntary. In the Bronx, Brooklyn, and Manhattan, you either had to join or become a target. I used to visit my cousin in Spanish Harlem. There I'd find all the romance a ten-year-old could wish for: tough gang, pretty girls, great parties. Sex was in the air, and so was fast living. In Queens we had gangs like the Spiral Sisters—Catholic-school girls who beat up boys in younger grades—while Manhattan had the Tomahawks and Savage Skulls, who'd beat up anyone, regardless of age, sex, or religious or political inclination.

I got arrested a few times, but only for stupid things: once for truancy, once for going off on a cop (always a big-mouth, I wouldn't let him have the last word), and once for breaking into a subway conductor's booth with a friend and commandeering the intercom. Some of my friends were in deeper trouble with the law for stealing cars and for dealing drugs. I wasn't that wild, but I always wanted to hang out with the really cool, hardened street fighters. I was a gangster wannabe.

At about that time I was voted Most Talkative in high school. (I wasn't politically organized enough to win Most Funny.) I spent most of tenth grade in the dean's office, inventing excuses and promising to mend my evil ways. My English teacher, Miss Ross, and my history teacher, Miss Singer, encouraged my performance ability subliminally by allowing me to wreak havoc in their classrooms. But it was my math teacher, Mr. Zufa, who actually suggested I take up comedy. The idea of studying acting sounded good to me, so I went to the Yellow Pages and looked up drama schools. I first tried out Sylvia Leigh's

Showcase Theater. Sylvia Leigh thought she was Blanche DuBois. She had an affected accent and was always dimming the lights around her. She had us do lots of speech exercises and script analysis.

My first acting-school scene was an Oscar-award performance if I do say so myself: *Dino*, the wiry troubled street youth—Sal Mineo had done it as a teleplay. I then got offers from New York University student filmmakers, who in my mind had the stature of Coppola. But after that initial success, my performances at the school sucked. "How?" you ask? Don't ask! Let's just say I've been chasing that high ever since.

At this point I realized a successful acting career requires serious commitment, so I decided to become a student-aholic. I studied my craft at NYU, the Strasberg Institute, HB Studio, and with Ken Eulo. Finally, I was cast in the starring role of a critically acclaimed student film called *Five Out of Six*. That got me an audition for *Miami Vice*, where I had a recurring role as a cocaine Mafia prince. If there had been an acting police on *Miami Vice*, I would've been arrested on too many counts. Then I was in two plays at The Public Theater in the East Village. Joseph Papp would tutor me in Shakespearean pentameter before my entrance as Puck. But I felt Puck to be too confining for my acting style. So I went wild. And I'm certain my unique interpretation destroyed *A Midsummer Night's Dream* for many a neophyte. Sorry, Bill.

From there followed a string of movie roles, playing the drug pusher/terrorist/immigrant/gigolo stereotype Latino: in *Revenge* I'm a gun-toting Mexican lackey; in *Die Hard 2* I'm a subliminal terrorist— you have to freeze-frame to catch what's left of me post editing; in *Regarding Henry* I'm the mugger. I have particularly fond memories of my first big film, *Casualties of War*, in which I played the silent minority— and I do mean silent! As the token Hispanic, I had very few lines and was meant to be part of the background. Instead, I gave the best face-gesticulating performance of my life. Fortunately, Brian De Palma never caught me enlarging my role, so I got away with it.

In the meantime, I was writing jokes for a children's theater company called the Off-Center Theatre, trying to juice up my parts in the various children's classics they presented. My Jack in the Beanstalk was a scam artist who tried to rip off the giant by making him shoot craps for the goose, play three-card monte for the harp, and toss a coin for his wife. Either the children were bused to the theater or the company traveled to Harlem and Spanish Harlem to perform in public schools and community centers. It was the highlight of my life. No other acting job, before or since, has given me so much satisfaction. The kids enjoyed it almost as much as I did. Inspired by their honest and uninhibited responses, I couldn't control myself and ended up stealing every scene.

I then joined the improv group First Amendment for a stint and found out that most improv is *not* improv, but sort of a script with a lot of blanks. Around this time I began serious work on my first one-man play. I performed twenty-minute pieces at legendary performance art spaces: P.S. 122, Dixon Place, and the Comedy Cellar. I took the point of view of what would have happened if Hispanics had a hand in history. I did a detective story with a Latino shamus hunting down the murderer of the Messiah. The Lord had been done in by the Mob because he was muscling in on their territory. He wanted to take gambling out of the temples and get rid of Mary Magdalene's pimp. He was getting wine from stones and not giving the Organization a percentage. So the gumshoe goes to Long Island and talks to Joseph and Mary Cohen. Then he goes down to Little Italy and talks to some wise guys till he meets up with Judas who has a contract out for him. They shoot it out and, of course, our hero wins and lives. There are eight million stories in New York and this has been one of them. The reception was overwhelming. I knew I had found myself, had arrived into my own. After a few more forgotten films, *Mambo Mouth* was conceived, and the rest is history—or press.

Mambo Mouth came to me as I was fighting very strenuously with my girlfriend of the moment back in August 1989. Adversity is my inspiration. I wrote the pieces, tried them out in the clubs downtown, and then took them to Wynn Handman, who was instrumental in my believing in my work. He helped me shape the pieces and then did the greatest thing ever: He introduced me to Peter Askin, the Scorsese to my De Niro.

Mambo Mouth is a combination cathartic purge of popular Latin media-types and my own personal take on street prototypes and wan-nabes. Some reviewers and members of the press insinuated that I was perpetuating stereotypes rather than lambasting them. I'm not going to defend my work because it's not my job—it's my mother's. But if my years of performing comedy have taught me anything, it's that you've got to be strong to make fun of yourself. In creating *Mambo Mouth*, I felt that mocking the Latin community was one of the most radical ways to empower it. I love the world I come from, and only because I do can I poke fun at it. Like Latin life itself, *Mambo Mouth* is harsh, graphic, funny—and at the same time tragic, desper-ate, and painfully raw. No stereotype could contain the pressure of all those explosive, conflicting emotions.

But enough about me. Now read my work.

GLOSSARY OF

FOREIGN TERMS

adiós: good-bye; later

arrigato: (Japanese) thank you

arroz con pollo circuit: chicken and rice circuit

arroz con pollo thighs: chicken and rice thighs

Ay, coño!: Oh, damn!

Ay coño, yo quiero perder control, ser lo que soy, ayudame, mamacita, estoy jodido, quiero bailar y gozar: Oh damn, I want to lose control, be wild, help me, mommy, I'm fucked, I want to dance and have fun.

Ay, Dios mío de misericordia, mi culpa: Oh! God of mercy, my fault.

Ay, fo: Euuu, yuck, eekie, poo, nasty

Ay, gracias, Papi! Gracias!: Oh! Thank you, darling! Thanks!

Ay, he was bien de groovy, tú sabes? Casi que me muero: Damn, he was very groovy, you know? To die for.

Ay, mira, precioso: Hey, look, precious

Ay, Perdóna: Damn! I'm sorry.

baboso: drooler, slimy

bendito: poor thing

bizcocho: pussy, beaver

bodega: grocery store

bruto: stupid

bubeleh: (Yiddish) Term of endearment meaning darling, honey,
sweetheart, little doll.

cabeza: head

cabrón: bastard

**cabrón, idiota, medio-malparido, cagado, pedazo de mierda envuelto,
baboso, bobo:** bastard, idiot, blue baby, dirty butt, wrapped-up
piece of shit, drooler, dope

católico: Catholic

Chaito, señor policía: Good-bye, Mr. Policeman.

chucawala: (Chicanoism) baby daughter

cocotazo: noogie

cojones: balls

coño: our equivalent of *damn* and has as many meanings

coño imbécil: damn imbecile

cuchifrito: deep-fried turnovers

culo: ass; butt; rump

desgraciado: ungrateful (but stronger)

desgraciado, bruto pendejo, que nunca sirvió para nada: ungrateful,
stupid dummy, that never did anything worthwhile

Dozo ohairi kudusai: (Japanese) Please come in.

el mundo de "cheap thrills y expensive regrets": the world of cheap thrills and expensive regrets

en la otra: in the other

ése: (Chicanoism) meaning dude; bud; guy; fellow; homey

gracias: thank you

Gracias, chico: Thanks, kid.

Gracias, pendejita: Thank you, little dummy.

Hai!: (Japanese) Yes; uh-huh; I hear ya.

Hasta la próxima. Epa!: Until the next time. Funky!

hermanos: brothers

hijo de puta: son of a whore

Hola, Abuelita: What's up, Grandma?

Hola! Epa!: (said while dancing) Wow! Funky! Groovy!

Hola, Mamá, cómo esta?: What's up, moms? How's things?

Hola, Negrito: What's up, my little dark one?

Hola, Ramón!: Hey, Ramon!

idiota: (this one is obvious) idiot

In your culo, puto maricón sucio: In your ass, dirty faggot fucker

kibitzing: (Yiddish) to putz around

kine-ahora: (Yiddish) Expression used to show one's praises are genuine and not contaminated by envy.

Konichi-wa: (Japanese) Hello.

Latina puta-bitch: Latina whore-bitch

Los latinos debemos ser unidos y jamás seremos vencidos: Latinos united, we'll never be divided.

mamis: babes; foxes; honeys; chicks

manos en la caca: hands in the shit

Mazel tov: (Yiddish) Good luck.

Mi culpa, señor. Que sufrimiento, ay!: My fault, lord. What suffering, oh!

mija: my daughter, my darling

mijo: my son, my darling

mira: look

Mira, mira! Policía, policía, please! Ayuda, socorro, socorro!: Look, hey! Police, police, please! Help, save me, save me!

Miss Masoquista: Miss Masochist

Ms. Caca de Toro: Ms. Bullshit

Nada. Bruto pendejo idiota: Nothing. Stupid, dummy, idiot

nena: girlfriend

No más, no más: No more, no more (Duran said this once before being pummeled by Sugar Ray)

número uno: number one

Olé!: Spanish expletive meaning something like Way to go!

Orale!: (Chicanoism) What's up?

Orale, gabacho pendejo: Waz up, dumb whitey?

Pa' fuera, pa' fuera, sucio demonio, coco inmundo, ayudame. Diosito!: Get out, get out, dirty demon, heinous bogeyman, help me my little Lord!

papi: daddy; baby; honey

pendejo: dummy (masculine); sometimes means pubic hair

Perdóna, señor policía: I'm sorry, Mr. Policeman.

pinga: dick; johnson; love stick; tube steak; hot beef injection

pipi: dick; weeny; wee-wee

Presentado por Telemundo de Paterson, New Jersey: Presented by
Teleworld from Paterson, New Jersey

primo: cousin

Primo, por favor dejeme ir que somos de la mismita sangre: Cuz,
please let me go, we are of the same blood.

puto: fucker

Qué te pasó?: What happened to you?

santero: a witch doctor or shaman of disputable powers; Santeria is
a religious practice in Latin countries taken from African voodoo, native South American folklore, and European Catholicism

santero mágico: magic man

Sayonara: (Japanese) Good-bye.

Se me paró!: Popped a woody!; Pop-up tent in my pants!: I got a
hard-on!

Shitsurei: (Japanese) Excuse me.

shmoozing: (Yiddish) rumors; idle talk; heart to heart prolonged
talk; gossip

"Sueños Calientes de Noches Frías y Pecados Católicos": "Hot
Dreams of Catholic Sins on Cold Nights"

**También presentado por Wine Cooler Sangría. La bebida preferida
pro los latinos de los nineties. El sabor del Caribe. Rico. Sauve:**
Also presented by Wine Cooler Blood-drink. The preferred drink
by the Latinos of the nineties. The taste of the Caribbean. Tasty.
Smooth.

Te lo corto!: I'll cut it off!

tetas: tits; mammaries; breasts; jammies; jugs

tortilla: Mexican pancakes

Tú eres mi moreno, mi macho: You are my brown one, my main man.

Tú eres un mugre, un moco, una cucaracha: You are dirt, a booger, a roach.

Yo te conozco: I know you.

Yo te quiero: I love you.

GLOSSARY OF

SLANG TERMS

buggin': losing it; going out of your mind; going crazy

crazy: an adjective denoting greatness

dissin': disrespecting

dope: great, awesome

dufus: dolt; big gangly one; goofy person

five-finger discount: stolen

flex: to use force; show off power

frontin': putting up a front; posing

goofin': just kidding, joking

ho: whore

ill: when something is very cool

motha: short for motherfucker

sweatin': bothering; having the hots for someone; on someone's
jock

AGAMEMNON

(Offstage: Agamemnon sings "Strangers in the Night.")

STAGE MANAGER: Yo, Mr. Agamemnon, you're live in thirty seconds.

(A robed Agamemnon enters from the back of the house and crosses onto the stage.)

AGAMEMNON: Coño, desgraciado, bruto pendejo, idiota!

Mr. Producer? Mr. Producer? I'm not going on. I refuse to go on. You know why? Because some unemployed actor is still in my dressing room. How do you expect me to prepare? I had to go into the alley, and this undesirable element—my wife—tried to talk to me. I need to visualize and concentrate because I am a method talk-show host.

Okay, okay. You don't have to get somebody else. I guess since you people came to see me, I owe you something.

(Preparation very dramatic.) Ay, Dios mío de misericordia, mi culpa. Mi culpa, señor. Que sufrimiento, ay! I am king of the Amazon jungle. *(Jungle sounds.)* Oooh, ooh, ooh, ooh! Aah, aah, aah, aah! *(Maniacal laughter, then hysterical crying.)* I can't do it, Mr. Producer. I don't feel it. You know, we are supposed to be a team, working for me, the star. It's just like my uncle Segismundo used to say: "The whole is the sum of the parts—and some of the parts don't seem to be working."

Difficult? Now you're calling me names? *(To audience:)* People, am I difficult? *(Waits for lukewarm response.)* Well, I must be then. You all sure are uppity for Off-Broadway prices. But people, I'm sorry you had to witness this debacle, but some people think they can treat me like a second-class citizen, like I'm some kind of Third World idiot, but what they don't realize is that I built myself from the arroz con pollo circuit to what I am today. And now HBO is here, and I'm moving my show right out of this pathetic little theater. Don't try to apologize now, desgraciado.

(Moves to stage rear and takes off robe, revealing leopard jockeys. Can I have a little privacy? I feel naked. *(Flexes as scrim descends. To silhouetted figure who appears to aid in dressing:)* Where have you been? Shmoozing and kibitzing again?

(Comes back around scrim. To audience:) And people, please don't sit on your hands tonight. God gave them to you for a reason. Use them. Gracias. *(Ducks back behind scrim until applause dies. Reap-*

pears.) I didn't say stop, did I? (*Ducks behind scrim.*) The more you give, the more you get! Well, I guess you're not going to get anything. Recession-type audience.

STAGE MANAGER: Five . . . four . . . three . . . two . . . Agamemnon, you're live!

(*Stage lights up, Agamemnon strides forward. He is dressed in a snazzy white suit, floral silk shirt unbuttoned at the neck to reveal gold chains, a white slouch hat, and black-and-white spectator shoes. He wears a few gold rings, a gold watch, a gold hoop earring, and a pencil-thin moustache. The only props are downstage: a stool and a small table, on which are a wine cooler, a cellular phone, a letter, a cue card, and a beam-balance, shielded from view.*)

Live, baby, I'm always live. *(Show's mambo theme music begins. Agamemnon signals audience to clap.)* Work with me, people. Hola! Epa! Stop it, you're spoiling me. Hola, hola, people, and welcome to *Naked Personalities*, the most dangerous show on public access TV. Where we take an uncensored look at your most favorite celebrity— me! That's right. And for the few of you who don't know me *(winks)*, my name is Agamemnon Jesús Roberto Rafael Rodrigo Papo Pablo Pacheco Pachuco del Valle del Río del Monte del Coño de su madre *(pauses to swig from wine cooler and signals to cut music)* López Sánchez Rodríguez Martinez Morales Mendoza y Mendoza.

But you can call me handsome. Why not? I deserve it. *(Searches audience.)* You women are probably asking yourselves, is he or isn't he? Well yes, ladies, I am . . . married. But don't lose hope because my lawyers are working on it, and pretty soon I'm going to be out and about. So beware . . . grrrrrrrr! *(Rolls r's.)* But remember, ladies, I'm not omnipresent—only omnipotent. Huh! *(Pelvic thrust.)*

Okay, people, I'd like to take a quick moment to say hello to all the women I have loved around the world, if you don't mind. How you doing? I miss you. 'Bye!

Okay, people. *(Puts down cooler, perches on stool.)* Let's open the show as we always do: by reading letters from women who want to be loved by me around the world. *(Picks up letter.)* And this first letter is from a woman who wants to be loved by me in El Salvador. Nice little underdeveloped country.

And it says: "Dear Mr. Agamemnon"—she respects me—"I am a Republican, single, Hispanic woman. Please come to my rescue. Invade me. Blockade me. Dick—tate me." *(To audience, pointing at letter:)* I didn't see that the line continued. "Spill your oils on my virginal beaches. Deplete me of my natural resources." Grrrrrrrr! "Be mine forever. Yours in Christ, Mimosa."

(Rises from stool, walks downstage. Pulls silver cigarette case out of pocket and removes cigarette, with flair, as he speaks.) Well, let's get something straight right off the top, okay, Mimosa? I don't get involved with my women. I'm a short-term guy. I don't fall in love, and I certainly won't marry you. *(Pulls silver lighter from pocket, flicks it open, and lights it across his thigh. Casually brings flame to cigarette.)* The only thing you can count on me for is satisfaction, gratification, ecstasy, passion, decadence, debauchery—and maybe kissing.

(Walks back to table and picks up another letter.) This next letter is from a woman who wants to be loved by me in Havana. That's my home town, by the way. Wait a minute—I already had her! Please, please, no repeats, ladies. No repeats on this show. *(To stage manager:)* Coño imbécil! I told you to read all my letters.

(To audience:) As a matter of fact, this Little Miss Charming here thought she was the last Coca-Cola in the desert. But people, let me tell you something—there's a difference between beauty and charm. A beautiful woman is one who I notice, but a charming woman is one who notices me.

Now we are going to start taking calls from our male viewers, so please call me on my chellular phone. Call me on the chellular because this is an opportunity for us Latino men to be vulnerable for one moment in our lives. So call me and lean your heads on my shoulder. Because that's what I'm here for. Whatever female problems you have, be it wife problems, mistress problems, two-women-at-a-time problems, prepubescent-nubile-girl problems, whatever the problem. Because if you have a woman in your life, you gotta be suffering from estrogen poisoning.

So dial 970-WEEP. This is your chance to bond and share. Come on, do two sixteen-ounce curls *(mimes weight-lifting)*, whatever it takes, and call me. I dare you. Last week I taught you how to save money by making love to yourselves. This week I'm going to teach you how to maximize your male potential with the mamis. Don't let the big cabeza tell the little cabeza what to do. *(Sips wine cooler.)* Okay, first caller. You're on the air.

CALLER #1: *(Voice is heard from offstage; Agamemnon listens, smoking:)* Orale! My name is Pepe, and I'm calling from Flushing.

AGAMEMNON: How ya doin', Pepe.

CALLER #1: I just want to say that I really like your show a lot.

AGAMEMNON: Gracias, chico. Gracias.

CALLER #1: My problem is that I'm dating a beautiful woman right now, and I've taken her out many times and bought her all kinds of gifts—

AGAMEMNON: You're in trouble already, my friend.

CALLER #1: We have a—what do you call it?—Christian relation-ship. But I want a lot more. What can you do for me?

AGAMEMNON: Pepe, you deserve a lot more. I know exactly what you are going through, because I have been there myself. This last Jezebel I was with did the exact same thing to me. I call this the Goldilocks Syndrome. That is when a fine blonde sexy mami comes into your life from nowhere, and suddenly she's eating all your food, messing up your fine upholstery, sleeping in your bed, and she's not giving you a damn thing. You got to get rid of that barracuda before she eats your heart raw.

Now let's take a look at Agamemnon's Scales of Justness. *(Reveals balance.)* Okay, Pepe, you've given her what? *(Places three weights into one pan of balance.)* Candy, flowers, and in your case, probably plastic slipcovers. And she's giving you what? *(Holds up uneven scale.)* Look at that! Nada. Bruto pendejo idiota.

You did it your way. Now do it Agamemnon's way. Take back the candy, the flowers, the plastic slipcovers. *(Removes weights from pan.)* Tell her you're going to call and don't. Mistreat her. Sleep around. *(Places all three weights in other pan of balance.)* And pretty soon those scales are gonna be on your side—okay, baby? Next caller, you're on the air.

CALLER #2: Hello, Agamemnon. My name is Angel, and I'm calling from Rikers. Yeah, I got this problem. This fine blonde sexy mami I've been getting visitation rights to isn't spending time with me anymore. She tells me that she's taking care of sick relatives, but I don't believe her. What can I do?

AGAMEMNON: Don't you ever believe them. Because I know exactly what you're going through. I have been there myself. This last piranha I was with did the exact same thing to me. I call this one the Little Red Riding Hood Syndrome. And that is when a fine blonde sexy mami is telling you that she's going to Granny's, but meanwhile she's in the woods being eaten by a wolf!

Stop being a eunuch. Get rid of her. And give me her number—I'll take care of her my way. Next caller, you're on the air.

CALLER #3: My name is Manny.

AGAMEMNON: Hello, sweetheart.

CALLER #3: This is a must-miss show on my list—

AGAMEMNON: I'm sorry to hear that.

CALLER #3: —because you are a misogynistic, homophobic, sexist, sorry sack of shit— *(Agamemnon hangs up.)*

AGAMEMNON: Well, thank you, Ms. Caca de Toro, for your cojones. But people, this is nothing. I'm already used to negativity. My father, Agamemnon Senior, made sure of that. Every night before he tucked me into bed, he'd say, "Agamemnon Junior, I can't believe that out of a hundred thousand sperm, you were the quickest." Oh, my father was a great source of comfort in my life. But where are you now? Eh, Papi? They caught you with your manos en la caca, and they sent you back to Cuba, desgraciado, bruto pendejo, que nunca sirvió para nada.

(Brings stool to foot of stage.) Bring the camera in closer. Tighten up to there. That's it. *(Strikes a pose.)* For all you Pepes and Angels and all you brothers and hermanos out there—if you learn only one thing from me tonight, it is my prayer that you don't fall in love with beautiful women. It's not worth it. Go for the ugly ones, then the loss won't mean as much.

Life gives you the test and then the lesson. That's how it works. I have loved my women too much, and they abused this privilege. There was a time when my love was this raw, all-consuming, back-breaking thing. This one woman—I would walk over hot briquets for her, make love like an endangered species, fight for her, make sacrifices—but for what? For what? So that one day she could step on my gentle trusting little heart and crush it. No más, no más, those days are over. As you get older, your heart shrivels up just like your cojones.

(Notices cue from stage manager.) Do you mind? I was trying to have a moment with my brothers. *(Picks up cue card, poses for camera, and reads in booming announcer's voice.)* Naked Personalities presentado por Telemundo de Paterson, New Jersey. Paterson, New Jersey. También *(picks up wine cooler)* presentado por Wine Cooler Sangría. Wine Cooler Sangría. La bebida preferida por los latinos de los nineties! El sabor del Caribe. Rico. Suave.

(Rises from stool, walks to center stage.) Okay, people. Without much further ado, it gives me great pleasure to introduce—oh, you knew it was coming, didn't you? That's right! The cultural part of the show. Because nobody is going to leave here saying that Agamemnon is uncultured.

(Moves furniture out of the way.) I would like to do a reenactment from a major motion picture that I once did, for which I won Best New Face in a Film Not Released. Because the director, who couldn't direct traffic, was an egomaniac and also the cameraman, and he forgot to take the cap off the lens. So all I have to show for it is my memory. *(Crushes cigarette with toe.)*

(Removes hat and gives it to silhouette dresser, upstage left.) But I'm going to give you a little taste. Or as they say in New York delis, a little schmear. *(Removes jacket and gives it to silhouette, upstage right.)* Gracias, pendejita.

It was called *(over-emoting) Sueños Calientes de Noches Frías y Pecados Católicos.* Which loosely translates *Nocturnal Emissions*—I mean, *Emotions.*

Imagine this, if you will . . . *(Hums "Strangers in the Night," looks around expectantly, yells)* imagine this, if you will! *(Lighting changes.)* Gracias.

Fade in. It is Florida. The Mecca for the retired, the refugee. God's waiting room. It's hot, oh yes, very hot, and the sun is setting. And *(mimes)* strolling down Miami Beach, picking up little broken seashells, is *(rolls r's)* RRRRRRRRebecca. And she's hot too. But she's also old and leathery and wrinkly—but American, oh yes, very American.

And just like her horoscope predicted, awaits me—RRRRRRRRamón, the Cuban cabana boy. And I'm sweeping the sand *(mimes),* closing the umbrellas. And I'm dark, devilish, desperate *(crosses himself),* Católico, and illegal, oh yes, very illegal.

Music swells. Romance is in the air. *(Conks salsa music and dances.)* They do the dance. The "I Want Something for Nothing" dance. *(Conks and dances.)*

RRRRamón holds her age-spotted, quivering, gelatinous, buttless body in his arms. *(Mimes dancing, holding one hand upright to simulate Rebecca's face.)* She presses against his alien Amazonian manroot. *(Gyrates hips.)* She wants fulfillment. She wants sin.

Close-up. *(Makes frame around face with hands.)* I am that sin. I am that forbidden, primitive, savage Caribbean lust-quencher. Extreme close-up. *(Smaller hand frame. Aside:)* The camera loves me. *(Back in frame.)* She's my chance, my dream, my opportunity. *(Aside:)* My green card. *(Drops frame.)* But people, people—I know that if I unleash just one drop of my Latino man-milk, she's gonna drop me like some empty jar of Porcelana. Boom!

(Conks and dances.) So we play the cat-and-spouse game. I penetrate her—with my glare. She gives me a look that I can feel in my hip pocket. Dolly shot. *(Mimes cameraman on dolly, smoothly crossing stage, crouched low. Then returns to mime of conversation with hand as Rebecca.)* She calls me Chocolate Eyes. I call her Albino Beauty. She calls me her greasy, treacherous raven. I call her *(licks fingers and yanks her imaginary hair)* Grandmother!

She is on fire—I can feel that hot blood pounding through her varicose veins. She says to me *(Spanish spoken with tacky American accent)*, "Yo te quiero. Tú eres mi moreno, mi macho." I say to her, "Please don't ruin my language." She demands satisfaction. I hold out for authentifisicisicisication.

Oh—she is outraged! No one has ever talked to her that way. She calls me he-slut. I call her Aryan whore. She calls me ethnic beast. I call her bitch-goddess. She slaps me! *(Shrinks back.)* I kiss her. *(Kisses hand.)* She slaps me again! *(Shrinks back.)* I kiss her again. *(Kisses hand.)* She kisses me. I slap her! *(Claps hands together loudly.)*

We are at an impasse! She won't naturalize. I won't fertilize. She won't legitimate, I'm not going to consummate. Cut!

The idiota pendejo director ran out of film at that point, so I can't tell you no more. I can tell you I never got my green card. But I can also tell you that she never got any— *(Hand gestures sex.)*

(Notices stage manager signaling.) Ay, coño! That's all the time we have for today. I didn't realize—we were having such a good time. Okay, people, please join me next week when my guest is going to be a very dear close personal friend of mine—me! Oh yes, but I'm also going to have a lot of other guests who are going to talk about how talented I am. And I'm also going to do another reenactment of a major network TV series I once did that was canceled—because, people, let me tell you something. I have a lot of enemies in Holly-wood. People who are jealous of my talent and my career.

Okay, okay. I'm going, I'm going. All right, people, thank you for joining me, and please don't drink and drive, okay? And please use protection. Because it is better to lose one minute of your life than to lose your life in one minute. Hasta la próxima. Epa! Huh!

(Theme song plays as Agamemnon exits upstage. Lights down.)

(Backstage lights up. Silhouetted figure dances upstage.)

LOCO LOUIE: Yo, where you going? Can I hang wich youse? . . .
Come on, why not? I'm a man, man. I just got some . . . Oh yeah?
Well, your mother is so stupid that she trips over the cordless
phone! . . . I didn't say nothin' . . . Have a good one. Peace. Yeah,
later.

*(Stage lights up. Enter Loco Louie, a loose-limbed, hyperactive kid,
around thirteen years old. He's wearing a red shortset with high-top
basketball sneakers, a yellow baseball cap with the visor bent straight up,
brass knuckles, a gold Batman medallion on a thick silver chain, and
a gold front tooth. He's carrying a blaring boom box and groovin' to a
kickin' lick.)*

(Yells to a window above audience.) Yo! Chonchi! *(Puts down box,
grooves some more.)* Chonchi! *(One more groove.)* Yo, smegma-breath,

come down man! Come down. I got something seriously dope to tell you, boy . . . Why not? Well, do your homework later . . . Okay, I'll wait for you. Hurry up. *(Seriously dope moves.)*

Hey, Chonchi, man, where you been? *(Turns off music.)* I've been looking everywhere for you, tithead! I even called your house—yup, yup—and your pops said you was in the bathroom buffin' the helmet. Ahhh! Busted! Ha, ha! You got busted! Ahhh! *(Cackles.)* Chill, I'm just goofin' wichoo. You buggin' and all that. Step off, Chonchi. Just step off.

Okay, look me up and down and see if you notice anything particularly different about me today. Take your time. Just look me up and down. *(Strikes homeboy gangster poses.)* What are you, blind or what, pendejo? I'm a man, man! Yup, I just got some! Ahhh! Go Loco! Go Loco! Go Loco! Go Loco! *(Serious dope groove.)*

Here comes Shanté, man. Let me do the talking, all right?

(Calls out to woman passing downstage.) Hey, yo, Mami! *(Kiss.)* How about a little tongue drill? *(Rolls out tongue and flicks it ferociously. She ignores him.)* Dyke!

(To Chonchi:) So where was I? Oh yeah—so check this out. I'm hanging by my lonesome, playing some hoops and shit, right? When Ninja comes along, and he's got this big box of caffeine pills that he got on a five-finger discount. And he tells me that it gives you the strength of ten men—if you know my meaning? You know my meaning! So I pop fifteen of those suckers right away, right? And I never even had coffee and shit.

So we're waiting for the shit to kick in, right? *(Whistles.)* And then one, two, three—*(Goes rigid.)* We are human hard-ons. We are horny as shit, boy. All we can think about is fucking. All we can talk about is fucking. We are fucked. So we say, "Fuck it, let's go fuck!"

So what do we do? We jets over to Nilda's Bodega and Bordello. We had to, cause all this has been buildin' inside us since we were born, and we can't get any to save our lives—and it hurts. Uh-unh, it ain't for lack of trying. You know me, Chonchi—I don't limit myself to things that breathe. Word! *(Bugs.)*

So we gets there, and we ring. *(Mimes ringing doorbell, makes buzzer sound.)* Nothing. So we rings again—nothing again. So we rings some more . . . nothing some more. So we figure they're sold out, right? But as we start to step, this big pockmarked, bald-headed, bad-breathed—*(Covers his mouth.)* Say it, don't spray it. I want the news, not the weather! Heh, heh, heh, heh!

I'm sorry. *(Wipes mouth on sleeve.)* So this big dufus opens the door. Hey, Chonchi, have you noticed how there's always somebody like that guarding those places? Yup, that's what happens to you when you get too much bizcocho! I'm serious, yup, yup.

So we follows him up these green crickety velvety stairs with mirrors all around. That's so you don't feel so alone when you come to do your nasty thing. And when we get to the top, there is this fine, crazy-ill, superdope, lick-my-chops, to-die-for mami! Oh my God, she is ferocious!

What? You know Nilda? Okay then, I guess she wasn't such a mami. Okay, I guess she wasn't so ferocious. Okay, so she was more like this—this—this fat fat fat fat fat gargoyle with big tetas and shit.

But I says to her anyways, I says, "Excuse me, we'd like some mamis, please." And she says, "You're lookin' at her." So me and Ninja looks at each other, and we're both thinkin', "Naaaahhhh!" And she says,

"It'll cost you thirty dollars each." Thirty dollars? For that? Well, all me and Ninja had was like five bucks between the two of us.

So I says to her, I says, "Excuse me, do you have somebody smaller?" And she says, "No, I'm all you need." And I says, "Fine, we'll come back next time and make reservations, all right?" And as we start to step, the big dufus grabs us, man. *(Reaches behind head and grabs shirt collar, standing on toes as if lifted from behind.)*

And she says, "I'mma take one of you anyway." So now me and Ninja got no choice but to choose. Odds—once, twice, three . . . *(Shoots. Then, with false bravado.)* I won! Psych! Go Loco! Go Loco! Go Loco! Go Loco! *(Grooves, with fading enthusiasm.)* Well, actually I lost.

Cause she takes me into this closet room with a mattress on the floor—and in a heartbeat she is butt-naked, man. And if she was fat then, she is triply colossal now! Yup, yup, she was like these—flaps! And these folds! *(Mimes.)* And these ripples and blobs of mocha ice cream stacked one on top of the other. She looked like this humongous caramel cloud!

And then she starts acting sexy and shit. *(Bats eyelashes and wiggles like a flirtatious young girl.)* Then she says to me, "I hope you're big! I hope you're real real real big!" Oh shit, Chonchi! That sent this ferocious bolt of fear to my Juanito Junior, you know what I'm saying? Like it almost climbed back inside of me. It was going, "Meep! Meep! Meep! Meep! Meep! Meep!" *(Whimpers and mimes the shriveling with finger.)*

Then she starts with, "Hurry, Papi! I want you. I want you now." So

I start to take off my clothes real slow, hoping she'd get done by herself. *(Mimes.)* But uh-unh, she still going shtrong.

And when I gets to my BVDs, I peeps in *(peeps)*, and my red-helmeted warrior is in a coma! So I starts making with the apologies right away: "This never happened to me before, lady. I got a lot on my mind. I got personal problems, homework, world hunger on my mind."

But she don't care. She just reaches over and goes, "Cuchi cuchi cuchi!" *(Finger mimes tickling.)* And one-two-three—*(Klock noise with tongue.)* Se me paró! That's right! One body, two minds, what can I say? Ah hah! *(Cackles with bravado.)* So then she condomizes me, right? And I bless myself, just like my mother taught me before entering danger. *(Crosses himself.)* And I close my eyes . . . *(With eyes closed, tries to find the edges of her body, reaching wider and wider.)* And I dives in.

Oh, Chonchi, man *(gyrates dreamingly)*, it is so soft . . . and warm . . . and plushhhh . . . that I begin humping like a maniac immediately. *(Wildly thrusts, arms still wide, eyes still closed.)* And she begins to laugh at me. So I begin to hump her a little more ferociously. And she laughs a little harder. So I really begin to drill her like a demon.

Well, now she's laughing so hard that she's almost crying, right. So I has to stop and ax her, "Excuse me, is it supposed to make you laugh like that?" And she says, "No, you got it in the wrong place!" *(Simulates Nilda's laughter.)* "Hua, hua, hua!" Oh my God, Chonchi, I felt just like I looked—stupid! I was lost in one of her flaps, man!

So what else could I do, but ax her, "Excuse me, could you please put me in the right place?" And she does. And oh my God, Chonchi man, if it was good then, it is heavenly now, boy! *(Closes eyes again.)* It is so gooey . . . and velvety . . . and safe. Then it hit me right there and then. I was born to fuck! I'm gonna fuck till I die and hopefully die fucking! And then I started to do all kinds of moves *(begins grooving and thrusting)* cause I saw it on Agamemnon's *Naked Personalities.* And she starts, "Ay, gracias, Papi! Gracias!" and her eyes roll right into the back of her head, and she begins to moan and groan. *(Groans à la Yosemite Sam.)* I thought she was going to die. But I can't stop myself, man. I'm on a mission. *(Thrusts rhythmically.)* I just keep going, and then one, two, three . . . *(Mimes orgasm with squish-squish-squish sounds.)* It's over. Just like that.

And I opens up my eyes—and she's this caramel soup! So I jump off her real quick, and I can't even look at her no more. And I do like the Santero said: *(mimes Santero ritual, brushing away spirits)* Pa' fuera, pa' fuera, pa' fuera, sucio demonio, coco inmundo, ayudame Diosito! And I shake all the evil away. I put on my clothes,

and I'm outta there like a bullet, man—whoosh! I don't turn back.

I did it! I did it, man! I'm a man! I'm experienced! Aah! *(Crows and grooves.)* Go Loco! Go Loco! Go Loco! Go Loco! And here I am, Chonchi. I came to share my triumph with you, cause you are my homey.

(Suddenly serious, stammering.) But between you and me—cause you're my homes—I was expecting my first time to be a little more . . . do you know what I'm saying? Like, I was hoping that it would be more . . . nah, it's not important. I'm a man now, and I don't gotta worry about shit like that no more.

Hey yo, Chonchi! You wanna be a man, too? My mom's got some money in her purse upstairs. Come on! Last one up is a dufus! I'll get you a discount, cause me and Nilda are tight like that now, boy. *(Crosses fingers.)* Let's bust a move! *(Turns on radio and begins dancing. Lights down.)*

(Backstage lights up. A cell door clangs shut. The silhouette of a hand-cuffed man is shoved onstage.)

ANGEL GARCIA: Get your hands off me, man! Get your hands off me! You're hurting me! Get your rug-wearing fucking guinea hands off me! Get the fuck off me. You're trying to incarcetize me for something I didn't do. *(A flash bulb pops offstage.)*

(Rubs one handcuffed hand across nose; it comes away bloody.) Look at that! You broke my nose, Desico! You didn't have to break my nose, man. *(Another flash.)* I'm not an animal. I'm a fucking human being! You got no respect . . . No, I'm not gonna go peaceably. And speaking of piece, how's your wife?

(Comes downstage.) Yeah, yeah, Desico, spare me the Miranda. You have the right to remain stupid!

(Stage lights up as Angel turns to face the audience. He is wearing black jeans, a black leather jacket, open, with a T-shirt beneath, silver rings and bracelets, and an earring. His nose is bleeding profusely, all over his upper lip and chin, and his hands are bloody from wiping his face. The only props are a stool with a telephone on it, downstage.)

(To audience:) Boo! What are you ass-snatchers staring at? Do you know me? I don't think so. What, you never seen someone busted before?

(Recognizes an inmate.) Hey, Ninja, is that you? Ninja Mutant Torres, what's a puto like you doin' in a fine institution like this? You can't even do your three-card monte right, stupid? . . . No, I didn't forget. We're in a recession, homes. I'm just trying to maximize my moneywise situation—then we'll agendicize . . . Yeah, in your culo, puto maricón sucio.

(Pleadingly working the cop.) Desi-coroonie, let me go, man! I swear I didn't do nothing. You're trying to incarcetize me for something I didn't do. I just had an argument with my woman, that's all. C'mon, you never disciplinify your women? I know you guidos, man. You're hot-headed just like we are.

Desico, I did not hit her! For your edification, I was just arguing with her, man—that's all. She had an accident. Come on, man—I love her! You know how much I love her? I was gonna breed with her. Now what does that tell you? . . . Well, your recollection does not matchesize with my recollection of the events.

(Confidential.) Check this out, Desico. Hear me out. I come home early, right? Boom. It's our anniversary, and I got some flowers, right? Boom. And I hear these suspicious noises, right? I know what's going on, but I can't believe she's that stupid to play me like that. Boom. I open up the bathroom door, and she's got my homeboy on top of her. Boom, boom, boom! You see what I'm saying?

That's right, a special romantic other. What am I supposed to do—sit there and ref? That's my woman, man! I love her so much, I'm gonna kick her ass. *(Punches wall. Then, under his breath:)* I'm not gonna let it get to me. Nothing's gonna get to me.

(Turns and combs hair.) You think you're gonna get to me, Desico? I don't think so. You're just a pimple on my ass. A fart in the wind. You know what you are? Tú eres un mugre, un moco, una cucaracha. You see this? *(Spits.)* That's you. That's me. *(Points to exit.)* That's you. That's right. You couldn't even beat your own dick. Oh, you like that one, huh, Ninja? *(Tries to soothe furious cop.)* I wasn't dissin' you. I was just goofin'. That's the problem with you cops, you got no sense of humor.

(Spies phone.) C'mon, Desico, man. I know my rights. I got the right to call my people. Don't try to dispriviligize me, officeroonie. *(Plays to grab phone.)* Well, fuck you very much.

(Lifts receiver and dials. Wipes nose as he waits.) Hola, Negrito, how you doing, Papa? Are you all right? . . . No, I'm okay too . . . No, Daddy can't tuck you in tonight, Papi. I got a lot of business to take care of. Could you go put your Mommy on the phone for me, please? . . . No, I don't want to talk to your dog. Just put Mommy on . . . Okay, okay, okay. Woof, woof, woof. Now go put Mommy on, all right?

(Holds hand over mouthpiece and addresses the cop.) Desico, man, I'm going to be out of here faster than a virgin running from John Holmes.

(Back to phone.) What do you mean she's not home? Mira, I just heard her telling you to say she's not home! Tell her to get on the phone . . . She doesn't want to talk to me? Negrito, put the phone up to Mommy. Go ahead, mijo. G'head.

ROSANNA, I KNOW YOU'RE THERE! YOU FUCKING DISRESPECTED ME! YOU SAY YOU'RE MINE, AND THEN YOU GO

AND PLAY ME LIKE THAT? AFTER ALL I DID FOR YOU? YOU
GET ON THAT PHONE RIGHT NOW!

She still doesn't want to talk to me? Okay then, Negrito, you know
what you do? You go over and tell Mommy that it's her fault that Daddy's in jail . . . No, Papa, don't tell her that. Tell her I'm sorry
and that I love her and that my life is nothing without her—hello?
Hello? Fucking stillborn, man! *(Slams receiver into cradle.)* Yeah, I
should've drowned that little sucker when I had the chance, huh,
Ninja?

(Wheedling.) Give me a chance, Desicoroonie. I won't charge it to
you. Besides *(picks up receiver)* this black mami I'm calling is so fine,
I would lick the dick of the last guy who fucked her just to get a taste
of that papaya juice. *(Dials.)*

(Into phone.) Hello, Shanté? How you doin', Mami? . . . Oh, baby
(suave and seductive), you sound so good, I swear to God you do. You
sound good enough to eat . . . It's Angel. Angel Garcia . . . The guy
who wears the leopard jockeys? . . . Yeah, that Angel. That's better.
Now listen, I'm in jail and I need you to post . . . No, not Yale. Jail!
Jail! J-A-I . . . That's very funny. Tee-hee, tee-hee. Now come on, I
don't have time to play games wichoo, all right? Listen, I need you
to post bail for me at the hundred-tenth precinct . . . Why not? . . .
Oh, my God! I did not say "Rosanna, Rosanna" during sex. I said . . .
"Hosanna! Hosanna in the highest," in my big moment. I was just
getting into it, baby. You musta misfuckinunderstood . . . I didn't
do no Rosanna. I don't even know a Rosanna . . . She called you?
When?

Oh baby, oh woman. Oh, woman, please, please, woman . . . Listen, my little ebony princess. Lovewise, I know I'm poison, okay? I know I'm poison, Mami! Just cause a man loves, doesn't mean he knows how to love. You know, when I was born, my mother was in labor for three days. Now what does that tell you? . . . Yeah, even then I was causing women pain. Go ahead and kick me when I'm down! Go ahead and call me names if it'll make you feel better. Express yourself.

(Holds receiver away from ear, then tries to calm her again.) So, are you done? Are you done? . . . No, I'll just wait here till you're done, cause I got no place to go . . . Listen, woman! Listen! If you're talking, you're not listening . . . That's it! If I'm not out of here by midnight, you're never gonna see me again, and it's gonna be your fucking fault! . . . Come on, baby, don't make me say shit I don't mean. *(Turns upstage to keep cop from hearing next lines.)* You know I love you. And that my life is nothing without you . . . Hello? Hello?

(To cop:) Hey, Desico, your phone's busted! I got cut off right in the middle of my conversation, man!

Come on, why you sweatin' me? Why you frontin' like that? I still haven't been connectitized. Give me a chance. *(Conspiratorial.)* I'll take care of you, I promise. I'll work something out. *(Threatening.)* Don't flex on me, cause I'll call my father and you'll find yourself hamburgerfied. Don't play me, cause I got more guts than a

slaughterhouse. You'll find yourself wearing a concrete hat. I'll give you a Colombian necktie! *(Dials.)* Wrap that shit right around your neck, motherfuck—

(Into phone.) Hello? . . . Yeah, hello. Ah, can I speak to my mom, please? . . . No, man, I don't want to talk to you right now. Could you just put my mom on? . . . Are you deaf? I said I don't want to talk to you! . . . No, man, you're not my father. Just put her on!

Hola, Mamá, cómo esta? . . . Oh God, Mom, I'm so glad to hear your voice, you don't know! . . . It's your little Angel . . . No, I don't want anything. Look, I'm just calling from the hundred-tenth precinct to see how you're doing, that's all! . . . Why you get so suspicious every time I call you?

Mom, are you drinking? *(Pain creeps into his voice.)* Oh—see—Ma, don't—don't do that drinking shit. You told me you weren't going to drink no more . . . Well, then, stop listening to those stupid Julio Iglesias records if they make you cry . . . All right, Mom, I'm going to be straight up with you. Yeah, I got into a little trouble. I hate to ask you, but can you come and get me at the hundred-tenth precinct? . . . I promise you I'll change. This is the last time. I swear this will never happen again. Now, can you just come down to the hundred-tenth precinct, please?

She called you? What did she say? . . . Don't listen to her, Mom. I did not hit her, Mom. She's a fucking liar, Mom! Don't believe her . . . Yeah, but did she tell you what she did to me? . . . Okay, Mom, I don't have time. I have a lot of business to take care of . . . Okay, okay, it'll never happen again, I promise. Now can you just come down and get me?

Mom, no, don't put Grandma on now! Don't put—(*Sighs.*) . . . Hola, Abuelita, how you doin'? How's your hip? . . . Okay, could you put my mom back on, please? . . . Abuelita, the devil had nothing to do with it . . . I don't really care what the Bible has to say, just put Mom back on . . . What do you mean, God has the last laugh? What kind of thing is that to say to somebody? Get off the phone!

Mom, don't ever put her on again. Now can you come down to the hundred-tenth precinct and get me out of here? . . . It's like five stops on the subway . . . It's not dangerous, I take the subway every fucking day! . . . I'm sorry, I'll never curse again, all right? Just make that asshole come with you!

It's the last time I'll ever ask anything of you again, I promise. I'm gonna change . . . No, Mom, I gotta get out of here . . . No, Mom, don't leave me here. (*Voice begins to crack as he becomes visibly upset.*) Don't listen to him. Why you always got to listen to him? Why don't you listen to me for a change? You owe me. You gave birth to me . . . I don't care if I'm yelling at you, because you never cared for me, that's why! Cause the only time you fucking cared for me was when you had nobody else, that's when you fucking cared for me! . . . Oh, yeah, Ma, watchoo do for me? What? Let him beat me every fucking day of my life, is that what you did for me? (*Sighs.*) Now you're going to do that crying shit on me. You're going to do that crying shit.

(*Holds receiver away and tries to compose himself.*) Shh. Shh . . . All right, Mom. Just forget it, okay? Don't come . . . Yeah. I'll be fine . . . No, I understand. Look, Mom, I got to go, okay? . . . Yeah, I know you love me. I know you love me. 'Bye. (*Almost hangs up, then puts phone back to his ear.*) Yo, Ma? . . . Yeah, if anything happens to me, it's gonna be your fault! (*Slams receiver down.*)

All right, Desico. Come on, man! *(Holds cuffed hands above his head.)* This is your big opportunity. So why don't you hurry up and lock me up, man?

I never needed nobody. Cause I got more guts than a slaughter-house, that's why. Yo, Desico! You know what I want for breakfast, man? I want freshly squeezed OJ, I want Canadian bacon, and I want a Spanish omelette, man! That's right, I want you to make it nice and runny. I'm gonna Spanishify you, man!

I never needed nobody. *(Looks around.)* I could work this. I could work from here. I could definitely make this my office.

(Lights down.)

(The stage is dark. A backstage light reveals the silhouette of a man wearing jeans and a T-shirt standing in a doorway.)

PEPE: Excuse me, ése, I just got this gift certificate in the mail saying that I was entitled to gifts and prizes and possibly money if I came to La Guardia Airport? *(Comes downstage.)* Oh sure, the name is Pepe. Pepe Vásquez. *(Panics.)* Orale, what are you doing? You're making a big mistake! *(Lights up. Pepe stands center stage, holding a grille of prison bars in front of his face.)*

I'm not Mexican! I'm Swedish! No, you've never seen me before. Sure I look familiar—all Swedish people look alike. *(Gibberish in Swedish accent.)* Uta Häagen, Häagen Däazen, Frusen Glädjé, Nina Häagen . . .

Okay. Did I say Swedish? I meant Irish—yeah, black Irish! *(Singsongy Irish accent).* Toy ti-toy ti-toy. Oh, Lucky Charms, they're magically delicious! Pink hearts, green clovers, yellow moons. What time is it? Oh, Jesus, Joseph, and Mary! It's cabbage and corned beef time—let me go!

Okay. (*Confessional.*) You got me. I'm not Swedish and I'm not Irish. You probably guessed it already—I'm Israeli! Mazel tov, bubeleh (*Jackie Mason schtick.*) Come on, kine-ahora, open up the door. I'll walk out, you'll lock the door, you won't miss me, I'll send you a postcard . . .

Orale, gabacho pendejo. I'm American, man. I was born right here in Flushing. Well, sure I sound Mexican. I was raised by a Mexican nanny. Doesn't everybody have a Maria Consuelo?

As a matter of fact, I got proof right here that I'm American. I got two tickets to the Mets game. Yeah, Gooden's pitching. Come on, I'm late. Orale, ése. Is it money? It's always money. (*Conspiratorially.*) Well, I got a lot of money. I just don't have it on me. But I know where to get it.

Orale, ése. Tell me, where did your people come from? Santo Domingo? Orale, we're related! We're cousins! Tell me, what's your last name? Rivera? Rivera! That's my mother's maiden name! What a coinky dinky. Hermano, cousin, brother, primo, por favor dejeme ir que somos de la mismita sangre. Los latinos debemos ser unidos y jamás seremos vencidos.

Oh, you don't understand, huh? You're a coconut. (*Angry.*) Brown on the outside, but white on the inside. Why don't you do something for your people for a change and let me out of here?

Okay, I'm sorry, cuz. (*Apologetic.*) Come here. Mira, mijito, I got all my family here. I got my wife and daughter. And my daughter, she's in the hospital. She's a preemie with double pneumonia and asthma. And if you deport me, who's gonna take care of my little chucawala?

Come on, ése. It's not like I'm stealing or living off of you good people's taxes. I'm doing the shit jobs that Americans don't want. *(Anger builds again.)* Tell me, who the hell wants to work for two twenty-five an hour picking toxic pesticide-coated grapes? I'll give you a tip: Don't eat them.

Orale, you Americans act like you own this place, but we were here first. That's right, the Spaniards were here first. Ponce de León, Cortés, Vásquez, Cabeza de Vaca. If it's not true, then how come your country has all our names? Florida, California, Nevada, Arizona, Las Vegas, Los Angeles, San Bernardino, San Antonio, Santa Fe, Nueva York!

Tell you what I'm going to do. I'll let you stay if you let me go.

What are you so afraid of? I'm not a threat. I'm just here for the same reason that all your people came here for—in search of a better life, that's all.

(Leans away from grille, then comes back outraged.) Okay, go ahead and send me back. But who's going to clean for you? Because if we all stopped cleaning and said "adiós," we'd still be the same people, but you'd be dirty! Who's going to pick your chef salads? And who's going to make your guacamole? You need us more than we need you. Cause we're here revitalizing the American labor force!

Go ahead and try to keep us back. Because we're going to multiply and multiply *(thrusts hips)* so uncontrollably till we push you so far up, you'll be living in Canada! Oh, scary monsters, huh? You might have to learn a second language. Oh, the horror!

But don't worry, we won't deport you. We'll just let you clean our toilets. Yeah, we don't even hold grudges— we'll let you use rubber gloves.

Orale, I'm gonna miss you white people.

(Lights down.)

MANNY THE FANNY

(Dance music plays. Backstage light silhouettes Manny, voguing seductively. Music fades. A figure appears and drags her onstage. Manny has long orange hair and shiny lipstick to match. She wears a skin-tight hot-pink minidress, black patent-leather pumps, doorknocker earrings, and large jangly bracelets; has Walkman headphones around her neck; and carries a black evening bag.)

MANNY THE FANNY *(to figure:)* I didn't come here to eat your food. I wouldn't eat at Chez Greasy Spoon if it was the last food on earth! Whaddya think, this establishment's exclusive? I just came here to take a piss!

(Lights up.) Don't talk to me like that, you old pervert. Cause I'll read you from cover to cover and you'll never recover. *(Snaps.)*

You people come here, you gentrify the neighborhood, you kick us out, and then you won't let us use the bathroom? You can kiss my amber ass. *(Sticks ass out.)* Go ahead and kiss it. Kiss it. Kiss it! I dare you . . . Don't you dare, cause I'll come over there and slice your motherfucking pipi off! *(Pulls giant knife from purse.)* Te lo corto. I'm not playing wichoo.

(Moves toward audience. Yells to nearby cops.) Mira, mira! Policía, policía, please! Ayuda, socorro, socorro! There's a case of discrimination going on over here.

Well, shit, I would if you had one! Oink, oink, oink—oops! Perdóna, señor policía! I'm just playing wichoo.

Well, don't give me that butch look. Save it for the cow at home! Oops—was that me? Did I say that? Ay, perdóna. This girl's got a big mouth, but she knows how to use it! *(Snaps three times in the sign of Zorro.)* Chaito, señor policía. *(Blows kiss to departing cops.)* Baboso.

I gotta do número uno real bad. I need a date, I need a date! *(Spots potential customer.)* Mira, Papi! Papi . . . *(indignant)* Baboso!

(Sings and vogues.)

> Girlfriend, how could you let him treat you so bad?
> Girlfriend, you know you are the best thing he ever had . . .

(Spies another potential customer.) Csst, csst, csst *(as for dog).* *(Blows kiss and acts seductive.)* Ay, mira, precioso, mind if I say *wow!* Why don't you stop and say hello? I'm like white chocolate—none of the color, but all of the flavor! You're not from around here. Where you from? . . . Milwaukee? Ooh, I like foreigners! Do you have a bathroom in your hotel? . . . Then why don't you let Manny the Fanny show you a good time?

Well, excuse me, your royal blackness! *(Curtsies.)* Stuck-up latent homosexual! Fuck you, your daddy is a faggot and he likes it. I know— I had him! *(Snaps both hands.)* Go ahead, throw that bottle. But you better have good aim, cause if I'm not dead *(pulls knife from purse),* I'm gonna come over there and slice your motherfucking pipi off! *(Mimes.)* I'm not playing wichoo.

(Vogues and sings; spies friend down the street.) Csst, csst, csst, csst! *(Then very loud:)* PSSSSSSST! *(Stomps foot and screams.)*

Rosanna! *(Snaps three times.)* Rosanna! Mira, Rosanna, you flat-chested no-ass spicarella! You hear me calling you. Don't pretend you don't know me, girl. What do I look like, a hologram? You must have flunked your manners at the Copacabana School of Etiquette, Miss Très Beaucoup Faux Pas! *(Snaps.)*

What are you doing on this side of the planet, nena? I'm so glad to see you. I got so much to tell you! Last night I met this papi. Ay, he was bien de groovy, tú sabes? Casi que me muero.

What's a matter wichoo? Oh girl, you're always down. Don't tell me, I know—a terrible thing happened to you again last night. Nothing! Ouch! Ha, ha! *(Snaps and twirls.)* I'm sorry.

You know I'm cold-blooded. So malicious *(snap)* and delicious! *(Snap.)*

Look at me when I talk to you. Don't cover your face. Come on, what's a matter wichoo?

Ay! Dios mío! Ay, no. *(Cringes, hand to heart.)* I didn't know. I swear to God I didn't know. Bendito, poor fragile thing. Okay, take a deep breath and pull your sorry self together.

Qué te pasó? What happened to you? Rosanna, if you can't talk to me, who can you talk to? Angel did that to you? Ay, nena, you can't let my brother beat you like that. That no-good low-life with his forty-deuce mentality and Delancey Street sales pitch! I'd like to hurt him. I'd like to cut his motherfucking pipi off for you! *(Takes a deep breath.)* Ay, Dios mío. Look at you. You look like you got hit by a truck—and you weren't that good-looking to begin with, neither!

Ay, listen to me. Ay, fo! Mira, nena, I know exactly what you are going through, because I have been there myself. I was a pendeja too. A regular little Miss Masoquista. Just like those poor sick bitches you see across the street. *(To women across street:)* Yes, I'm talking to you! Ho! *(To Rosanna:)* Always hooked up with abusive pricks, that was moi. Because I thought getting slapped around and getting kicked upside my head was better than nothing, as long as there was somebody in my bed when I woke up in the morning. Because somewhere in this warped mind of mine, I just convinced myself that it was love. And from then on I was lost en el mundo de "cheap thrills y expensive regrets," tú sabes? Oh, don't go. Cause let me tell you, it gets even worse!

One day, I met this one dark prince. This guy who played me like a fine violin. Plucked my G-string just right and made me feel like everything was Disney. And this poor sick puppy put all of herself into this one guy, cause she heard wedding bells. So I gave him all my money, pawned all my possessions, and gave up a once-promising career as a cosmetologist at the Wilfred Academy of Beauté *(snaps)* just to send this Judas hijo de puta through night school.

But unbeknownst to me, he was just using me and taking all my money to entertain other bimbettes and laughing—laughing, mind you—at this poor lovesick freak behind her back. *(Sighs.)* But when I caught wind—and let me tell you, I did—Sleeping Beauty awoke! *(Cross snaps.)*

So, I came home early one night and I unscrewed all the bulbs *(mimes)* and hid in the closet with an iron in one hand and Krazy Glue en la otra. *(Mimes, eyes closed.)* And I waited.

Nine o'clock . . . ten o'clock . . . eleven o'clock . . . I thought he was never gonna come, right? But at exactly midnight, in sashays the Judas hijo de puta. Trying to turn the lights on and calling my name all lovey-dovey: "Oh, Manny? Manny, I got something for you. I got something for you." I got something for you, too, cabrón! And I just held my breath, cause this girl wasn't about to let his magic wand cast a spell on her again.

Then I heard his Florsheims get closer—and closer—and closer— and when he got to the closet door, I prayed for God to give me the strength and I popped out and conked him on the head with the iron. And on his way down, I undid his zipper, took out his big ol' pinga, put Krazy Glue up and down, and slapped it to his thigh. *(Mimes ever so daintily.)* Then I dragged the body out and locked the door. *(Wipes hands.)* Punishment accomplished, right! *(Snaps.)*

But when he came to—ay, Dios mío! He was screaming and crying, "I'm going to get you, Manny! I'm going to kill you! I'm going to beat you to death!" I knew then I'd done something wrong. *(Bites finger.)* But I didn't care no more. And do you know why, nena? *(Empowered.)* Because I took charge of my life. So I just flicked on the radio and drowned him out. *(Jumps into a routine.)*

> To be or not to be,
> That is the question.
> You've lied your last lie *(hands talk)*
> And I've cried my last cry. *(Wipes tear.)*
> You're out the door, baby! *(Points out and locks the door.)*
> There's other fish in the sea. *(Reels in fish.)*
> Olé! *(Grand finale of snaps.)*

So, you see what I'm telling you? Oh, I know I'm crazy. *(Tenderly.)* But life is too short to let people crush your world. But yo te conozco. I know you, Rosanna. You'll go home and he'll beat you and you'll let him beat you and you'll go through this love-hate hate-love thing till one day you're hiding in the closet with an iron in one hand and Krazy Glue en la otra.

But until that day, don't live on dreams. Because there are no Prince Charmings coming to save you. Just a lot of frogs. So you know what you do? You take your frog by his little green dick and you make him do what *you* wanna do. Because you are a Latina of the nineties. *(Snaps.)* Get with the program, mija! If it wasn't for a Spanish woman, Columbus woulda never discovered America. *(Double snap.)* Olé!

Now go ahead and get home before he beats you up for breathing. Take care of yourself, nenita. And call me. Call me, I'll get the message. Call me at Nilda's. Yeah, cause she wants me to play a practical joke on this little boy named Loco. *(Blows kiss.)* Chaito.

(Alone, looks skyward.) Oh God, please take care of her. *(Sings and vogues.)* Girlfriend, why do you let him treat you so bad? Girlfriend . . . ay, Dios mío, I need to do número uno so bad, I can taste it— please! *(Sucks in breath.)* Ay, Dios mío, I need a date. I need a date.

(Spies guy in midaudience.) Csst, csst, csst, csst, csst! *(Blows sexy kiss. Advances toward audience.)* Ay, mira, precioso, mind if I say *wow!*

(Lights down.)

(Backstage lights up. Latin music plays. A man and a woman are in silhouette. He takes her arm.)

INCA PRINCE: Come on, baby, let's go upstairs . . . What's the matter? I didn't go messin' around. I was just out drinkin' with the fellas. Come on, I'm gonna take you to paradise, baby . . . What? He's cryin'? What's he cryin' about? . . . All right. All right, I'll go talk to him. Stop bustin' my onions. Just go upstairs and wait for me. *(Stage lights up. Inca Prince enters, drunk. He wears a white tank top, jeans, and a bandana on his head with an Aztec medallion on the forehead. He weaves toward a small bed downstage.)* What do you mean I'm not gonna get any? Is that a threat or a promise? It wouldn't be the first time.

(To child in the bed:) Come on, Carlitos, I know you're not sleepin'— stop pretendin'. I wanna talk to you. Your mother isn't going to wait for me forever.

(Turns and shouts out window.) Hey, turn that goddamn music down! People are trying to sleep up here! *(Music gets louder.)* Ever since those goddamn Colombians moved in, nobody can get any sleep!

(Sits on the edge of the bed and addresses the child.) You're crying. What are you crying about? I got something for you. *(Pulls out Spiderman toy and sings.)* Spiderman, Spiderman . . . does whatever a spider can. Catches thieves just like flies, here comes the spider man. *(Plays with toy trying to get Carlitos's attention. The kid doesn't respond.)* I tried.

Why are you crying? . . . They called you a name? That's why you're crying? Don't you ever let me hear that somebody called you names and you didn't beat the motha! I taught you how to defend yourself. I taught you how to box. Do I have a son, or do I have a little daughter?

(Playful—almost trying to make up for what he just said.) You got nothing to be ashamed of. Don't you know you are a direct descendant of

the raven-eyed Inca god, Chibcha? Hark! We have the spirits of the ancients in our blood! You think I'm just a burn with an Incan head-dress, but you're wrong. I am authentic, seriously authentic. I'm the santero mágico, the magic man!

(*Really hams it up, trying to make the boy laugh.*) Oh, wait a minute—I'm getting a communication from above. Hmmm. What is that, O Great One? Hmmm. I should what? . . . Slow down—too much info . . . I should offer the world-secret lotion notion potion (*pulls bottle of booze from back pocket*) to this mortal? To this puny little mortal? This must be your lucky day, Carlitos! This potion was obtained by my great-great-great-cousin Julio La Brea Cahuenga Tahunga La Cienagea something or other. He was the great Aztec thief. All you have to do is give a little of this to the woman you crave, and she will perform the most unnatural and uncomfort-able acts you want. You'll appreciate this when you get a little older. (*Takes a swig.*)

We come from so many famous people, Carlitos. People who have done this and done that . . . Like who? Like who. Like Maria Consuelo Cleopatra . . . What, you didn't know she was Latina? Sure—as a matter of fact, Marc Antonio Rodríguez was madly in love with her.

And how about Guilliam Shakesperez? Yeah, Guilliam Shakesperez. He wrote some great stuff—*Romero y Julieta, Macho Do About Nothing, The Merchant of Venice-Zuela*. "Alas, alack, alook and a lick, hither, thither, fie, fie, fie . . ." You didn't know he was a quarter Latino? Oh, yeah. As a matter a fact, inside of every great person there's always a little Latino.

(Pointing bottle at Carlitos.) Hey, pay attention! Cause this is for your benefit. I already know this shit.

(Pulls bottle away from kid.) No, you can't have any. When you work hard all day at a job you don't like and are married and have kids, then you can drink all you want.

What did you call me? Don't worry, I'm not gonna hit you—I wanna know what you called me . . . Don't you ever talk to me like that.

You respect me! I'm your father! . . . Is that what they called me? Is that what you're crying about? Well, tomorrow I'm gonna go to school with you and you're gonna tell all your little friends that I'm the most famous has-been, coulda-been, woulda-been that they ever gonna meet.

(Stands up and mimes sportscaster, using bottle as mike and speaking in a booming voice.) In this corner, all the way from Avenue A, the un-

defeated lightweight champion of the Loisaida *(he flexes and poses),* the Inca Prince. Yeah! Yeah! *(As crowd would cheer. Then in normal voice.)* The babes tingled. The men admired me. I was handsome and sleek and in my prime. *(Poses bodybuilder style.)* The most powerful hands known to mankind.

I fought for the championship, Carlitos. We came at each other like two wild dogs. Left, right, left. *(Mimes.)* The first punch—I knew I had him. I knew I had him! By the end of the fifth, I came at him with everything. The crowd was roarin' for me! Upper cuts, combos, the whole nine.

When he went to his corner, I heard him say, "I don't know, Dad, but every time he hits me, it paralyzes me. It feels like his gloves are full of rocks!"

Of course it does, because I'm the Inca Prince. Yeah! I made his face look like raw meat. Knocked him and his father's dreams right out. *(Lunges.)*

At the end of the bout the ref comes over to shake my hand and takes my gloves and squeezes. *(More sober.)* He found the little rips, the little tears, and the missing padding. He took the fight away from me. It was mine, and he took it away from me. I could have won that fight on my own, but I thought, the sure thing, always go for the sure thing. I made a mistake—a big mistake—on the biggest night of my life. *(Primordial scream.)*

(Turns to Carlitos.) What's that? That's right. Spiderman, Spiderman—does whatever a spider can. Catches thieves . . . You know, Carlitos, when I was a puny kid just like yourself Spiderman was my biggest hero. Because he was just like me. Short, broke, but he had that Spidey sense and no one could touch him. And I used to pray all the time that when he took off that mask and costume, there'd be this little Spanish man in there. Of course, there never was.

So believe in yourself, because they can knock you down, but they can't knock you out. I love you, Carlitos, and that's the best I can give you. But if you don't go to sleep, I'm going to give you a big coco-tazo. Good night, little Inca Prince.

(To offstage:) I'm coming, woman. If you can't wait, then why don't you start without me?

(Lights down.)

(Japanese gong sounds. Audience sees silhouette of a man doing a low bow. Lights up as the Crossover King enters from behind the scrim. He wears a conservative gray suit, white shirt, muted silk tie, silk hanky in breast pocket, wing tips, and thick black-framed glasses, and he carries notes. His hair is slicked back and his movements are controlled. He walks to the lectern, center stage, and places the notes on the stand, beside a full glass of water. When he speaks—in a Japanese accent—his gestures are stiff. He pushes the bridge of his glasses with his index finger.)

CROSSOVER KING: Oh, yes, you in the right place. *(Arranges notes.)* The Crossover Seminar is about to begin, so hurry up and grab a seat. Hai! *(Violently bows head as he exclaims. Sips water.)*

Konichi-wa. Dozo ohairi kudusai. Hai! *(Jerks head.)* Welcome and welcome, Latino-sans, to the Crossover Seminar. Now, this could very well be the biggest investment of your entire life, so please hold your questions until the end. Hai! *(Jerks head, then sips water.)*

You too could be a crossover success. It's up to you *(points to an audience member)* and you *(points to another)*. This is purely a scientific method. There are no placebos or messy ointments.

Now, what exactly is a crossing over, you ask? That's a good question. Crossing over is the art of passing for someone that you are not in order to get something that you have not. Because there is no room in the corporate upscale world for flamboyant, fun-loving spicy people. So get used to it. I did.

Let's talk about the American mind made simple. Americans admire what? . . . Don't all volunteer at once. I have all day . . . Am I speaking a foreign language? Americans admire what? I'll give you a hint: It's green, you used to be able to buy things with it. *(Answer from audience: "Money.")* Arrigato! She is ready for the advanced course, but the rest of you have to stay. Yes, Americans admire money, but they also admire the appearance of having money. The more money you have, the more respect you're going to get. But if you can't have the money, you sure better look like you have it. Because America keeps sending you the subliminal and not-so-subliminal signals that without money you are inadequate.

Stop. *(Hits himself on the head.)* Stop hitting yourselves in the head and think for a moment. Why settle for being Latin trash? Why even settle for being American trash, when you could be so much more? So much more—like Japanese! This is a rich market to be harvested, Latino-sans. You alone have the choice: American *(holds right hand low, by hip)* . . . Japanese *(holds left hand high in the air)* . . . Japanese . . . American . . . good . . . bad . . . bad . . . good. You choose. Hai! *(Jerks head.)*

I'm going to share a little secret with you. You won't believe this *(confessional)*, but I was a Latino-san myself. *(Visibly ashamed.)* Yes, it's true. But with this easy-to-follow program, I have evolved and become a Japanese warrior. Very repressed, but also very successful.

I used to be loud and obnoxious, full of street mannerisms. Constantly holding my crotch for self-assurance. *(Mimes awkwardly.)* I would yell all the time, "Hola, Ramón! I just had a girl with tetas to here and culo out to there!" *(Mimes.)* But now I zen-out and only speak when I have something really important to say.

I used to not even be able to walk down the street and hear rhythmic percussion without my hips beginning to gyrate wildly and uncontrollably. *(Hips gyrate beneath lectern.)* But now I listen to Lite FM. And I hardly move at all—even when I want to. *(Sips water.)*

I used to be full of Latino macho braggadocio, disrespecting my women and wanting to start fights all the time. *(Picks audience member.)* Watchoo looking at? Watchoo looking at? You talking to me?

You talking to me? *(Steps out from behind lectern.)* I'll sucker-punch you, head-butt you, body-slam you, knock you to the ground, and spit in your eye. *(Suddenly all business again.)* Et cetera, et cetera, et cetera. *(Returns to lectern.)* Relax. It was just a dramatic re-creation. Hai! *(Jerks head.)*

But no more. Now all my aggression goes into beating up my business partners.

I know, a lot of you are thinking, "I don't need this. I don't see anything wrong with me. I like the way I am." Fine—but nobody cares what *you* think. It's what *they* think that counts.

(Sets up a projection screen.) Now, I'm going to accompany myself with some visual aids in order to more closely examine these cases of traditional stereotypicality. If you recognize yourself or loved ones, please do not panic. The Crossover King is here. Hai! *(Picks up projector remote from downstage.)* This is not for the squeamish, so be brave, Latino-sans, and face up.

Now, is your hair bleached to a color not found in nature? These are my cousins, the Henna sisters: Lizette, Annette, and Jeanette. They have a henna dependency from trying to be blonde sexy mamis. But I put them on a detox program, and I'm slowly easing them off the dyes and peroxides.

Do you wear Fourteenth Street doorknocker earrings, like my little sister, Yolanda? Those are dangerous! A big wind could come and knock her out and kill her. And you'd have another doorknocker-related death.

*Identities have been obscured to protect the unfortunate.

Do you make the streets your office?

Our photographer took this shot two weeks later and Miss Guzman was still there. Please get a life, Miss Guzman.

Oh, this is a special case. *(Ceremoniously takes collapsible pointer from breast pocket and unfolds it; uses to illustrate specific features on remaining slides.)* Are your clothes cutting off your circulation? Might you have the Aztec curse? *(To slide:)* Yes, Angela, you know what I'm talking about.

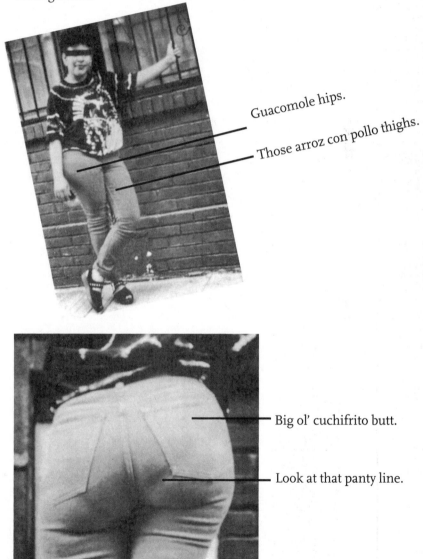

Guacomole hips.

Those arroz con pollo thighs.

Big ol' cuchifrito butt.

Look at that panty line.

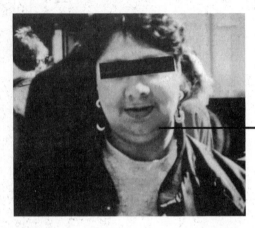

The dreaded tortilla chin

How many can you count? *(Uses pointer to count off at least four chins, then advances to black slide.)*

If you have developed any of these characteristics, you may have already become what Americans call, behind your back, the little, brown, roly-poly, Spanish, submissive, subservient, no-good Latina puta-bitch! Now let's not help perpetuate negative stereotypes. Only you can prevent this ugly misrepresentation.

I know some of you are thinking, "That's all very well and good, but what can that Crossover King really do for me? What is that little devil up to?" Stay with me.

Here we have my aunt, Rosa Herrera. She was a loud, gum-snapping, hairy-lipped, Bacardi-drinking, welfare-leeching, child-bearing, underachieving, no-good Latina puta-bitch. Oh, she was so loud! She would talk your head off all the time: "Did you see so-and-so? She's pregnant again. He'll never marry her now. Why buy the cow when you can get the milk for free? Blah, blah, blah. Yak, yak, yak."

But with our program, Rosa Herrera has become . . .

Rose Hara, the timid, self-disciplined, lonely, constipated workaholic. Her hair is a human color. No makeup to make her look like
some exotic tropical fish. No American don't-push-me-I-get-paid-by-
the-hour attitude. From head to toe she is a model of respectability.
Why, she could attend a party at a Tokyo Hilton and not even be told
that the servants' entrance is in back. She has crossed over nicely.
Hai!

Now for you men—or homeys, as you like to be called—don't think
I was going to forget you. I suggest you take special note. Awareness
is the first step to self-improvement.

Look at all that gold.

This is my cousin Hector, the drug dealer. Oh yes, he is hard and tough—but so are arithmetic and calculus!

It is better invested in a money market account than hung around his nefarious neck.

This is Tito Testosterones. He beat me up in the seventh grade—because I knew who my father was. Tito is the typical greasy, catfish-mustachioed, fake-gold-chain-wearing, beeper-carrying, polyester-loving, untrustworthy, horny, uncircumcised spic specimen. He will never get anywhere, except in a lineup.

(Addresses slide.) Look at me, Tito. Look at this success story now. *(Uses pointer on himself.)* Savile Row worsted tweed, Sulka Sulka tie, Varnet frames, Gucci shoes, Fortune–500 Ivy Leaguer that I've become. *(Turns to slide again, agitated.)* Look at me, Tito. I said look at me. *(Loses control completely.)* Cabrón, idiota, medio-malparido, cagado, pedazo de mierda envuelto, baboso, bobo . . . *(Struggles to regain composure.)* Shitsurei. *(Bows.)* Shitsurei. *(Bows.)* Excuse me. This never happened to me before. I had a little Latino relapse. *(Straightens clothes, smooths hair.)*

But our expert computer graphics team suggests that with only six months in our program, Tito could become . . .

Toshino, the quiet one! Well-dressed, manicured, somewhat anal retentive, but an overachiever who's ready to enter the job market at a drop of the value of the dollar. *(Clicks slides off and deposits remote downstage, then returns to lectern.)*

Once you have dulled your personality and have become lifeless and unimaginative, you are ready to reap the rewards of the corporate world. Don't wait for miracles. All it takes is a lot of restraint and a little bit of Japanese know-how.

(Incensed.) Now, I'm your Crossover King, and I'm going to help you to cross over. And if you don't like it, you can just kiss my yellow tail. Yes, I said it. Because we are going to own everything anyway. We are going to own your mother, your father, everybody, so you better cross over while you still can. It's nothing personal, just big busi-

ness. And we're going to take all our competition, and we're going to sucker-punch them, head-butt them, body-slam them . . . *(Shakes, sweats, and begins to fall apart.)* Ay coño, yo quiero perder control, ser lo que soy . . . ayudame, mamacita, estoy jodido, quiero bailar y gozar . . . *(Becomes completely unhinged, conking, tearing open shirt, and spewing forth a torrent of Spanish profanity.)*

(Tries desperately to control himself, clinging to lectern, and is finally able to gulp down some water. Pants and sweats.) Just kidding. Just kidding, like you American people say, just kidding. Well, being Latino need not be a handicap. Don't settle for affirmative action and tokenism. *(His feet begin mambo dancing beneath the lectern, while the rest of his body tries to hold still.)* Purge yourself of all ethnicity. *(His dancing feet take him out from behind the lectern. His upper body is still stiff.)* Well, that's all the time we have for tonight. Thank you for attending. *(Tries to control his legs, slaps his thighs.)* Remember, all it takes is a lot of restraint and a little . . . *(Bursts.)* Go Loco! Go Loco! Go Loco! *(Grooves.)*

Sayonara. Hai! *(Deep bow to audience.)*

(Lights down.)

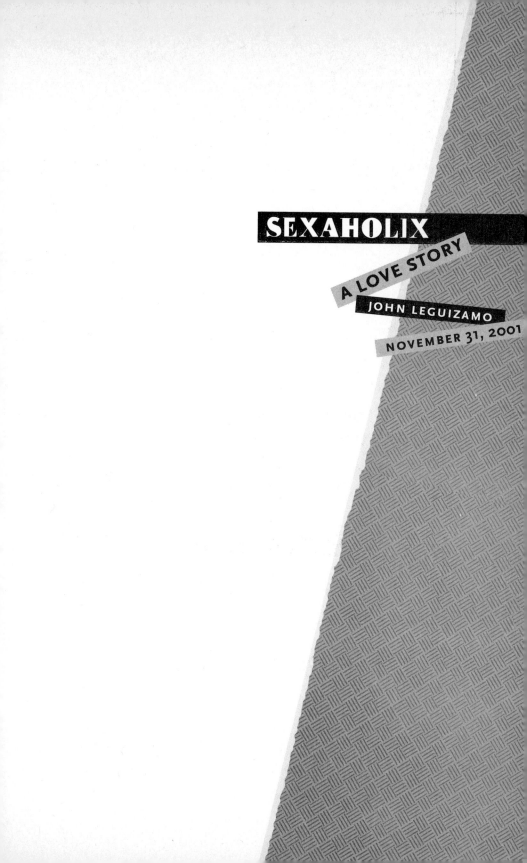

SEXAHOLIX

A LOVE STORY

JOHN LEGUIZAMO

NOVEMBER 31, 2001

Big Song. *John comes out dancing.)* Old school. High school. White school. Puerto Rican school *(break dance).* Colombian school *(ad-lib: not the college).* Mexican. Dominican. *(Put mic behind stool.)* Was up people! Talk to me, baby. Let me feel you. Cause we're gonna get nasty, we're gonna get raw, we're gonna get funky.

CAN A GIRL BE A BASTARD?

Cause this is my last chance to party cause I've got a daughter and a son ... (*dances*) and now I have everything but a life; (*dances*) no clubbin', no goofin', no sleep, no sanity. That's why I wrote this show so I could get the hell out of the house. (*Dances.*) But don't get me wrong I love my kids—I'm just gonna raise them a lot better than my parents raised me cause my parents damaged me but I forgive them cause it made me what I am today. But my kids don't need to be that successful. I remember when I was growing up my father was always saying ...

POPS: You kids are nothing but little retarded midgets that live in my house and don't pay rent.

And I know I'm gonna be different cause my kids are gonna pay rent. And my mom always used to say ...

MOMS: John, papi, I wanted to have an abortion but it was too late you were already in college.

And I thought I was doing a good job with my kids until one night I'm putting them to sleep and my daughter, Boogie, who's two, and my son, Little Man, who's eleven months younger. Yeah, Latin twins so what. I was horny. I couldn't wait the six months, aight. And my Boogie says . . .

BOOGIE: Daddy, can a girl be a bastard?

JOHN: Who said that to you?

BOOGIE: Grandma.

JOHN: Now, Boogie, you know I love your mother too much to marry her.

What? You don't know me . . .

JOHN: Boo, now go to sleep.

And I close the door and I hear her say . . .

BOOGIE: Just tell everybody we're adopted.

The little Judas brat, turning on me already (I might as well be myself she's gonna hate me anyway) when she doesn't need to worry cause her mother, my girlfriend . . . she and I are gonna stay together forever. Always in love, loyal and do you know why? Cause we're not married. That's why. *Sure Marriage came up. We talked about it.* We examined what we both brought to the table. She's Jewish, I'm not. She comes from money, I do too—now. She went to the best schools, I knew where they were. And we came to the same conclusion. We would leave each other in a heartbeat except—she's my other half. My true love. We were meant to be. We're like soulmates on permanent booty call.

And I'm not a bad father either. I give my kids everything private school, a big house, a Jamaican nanny . . .

JAMAICAN NANNY: Me want me smokes, Bun bun. Get me fatty
    for your nanny and if the cops come tell them it's your daddy's.
    (*Gibberish.*)

I even gave them a way into the white world. Cause they're Jewari-cans. Half Latin and half Jewish. So they'll be able to dance and balance their check books. (*Dance and balance check books.*) *"Credits, debits. Wepa."*

FRESH-AIR FUND

FIRST WHITE FAMILY

N ow, my introduction into the white world and another kind of family, happened when I was about nine years old cause my parents couldn't wait to get rid of me every summer so they'd send me to the Fresh-Air Fund. It's this organization that takes poor underprivileged inner city kids and sends them to a rich white family in the country for two weeks. And just when you're getting comfortable: Three meals a day, ketchup wasn't a vegetable. They snatch it away. So if you didn't know how poor you were now your ass really knows.

I went to brag to my homeys. We'd hang out on the same stoop every night. And it was Fucks Funny, Xerox, and English. Those were their tags. Fucks Funny, we called him that cause he had big ears like a rabbit and a bent dick . . . (Picture it on your own time).

FUCKS FUNNY: (*High nasal lateral lisp:*) Yo, man, they're gonna do mad experiments on you. You're gonna come back like circumcised and what not.

XEROX: (*Deep voice:*) Yeah, yeah, circumcised and what not yeah.

That was Xerox cause he repeats everything. And English we called him that cause spoke in the past tense cause he knew he had no future . . .

ENGLISH: (*Depressed:*) Yo, you go up there and you're gonna get lostededed. I'm gonna missededed you.

XEROX: Yeah, yeah, miss . . . los . . . what he said.

So I get on this Greyhound bus that takes me all the way to Vermont and I get off and this perfect white J. Crew family comes out complete with gin and tonics in the morning. And my Fresh-Air Father comes up to me . . .

POPS: (*Drunk. William F. Buckley:*) Oh, look, Marg, we got us a little Mexican. Would you like a drinkie-pooh, Jorgay?

JOHN: Yo, no offense mister but I'm ain't Mexican.

MOMS: (*A drunk, head shake.*) I do so love Cancún.

JOHN: Yo, Lady, what are you deaf? I just told you I ain't Mexican.

POPS: Calm down, Julio, we're going to buy you everything you've ever wanted.

JOHN: Pues, orale, vato. Can I get you a margarita?

And as we were leaving the town square, where all the FAF families would parade their ghetto prizes, I heard this mothers going off . . .

FRESH-AIR MOTHER #2: The Petersons have a real live junkie. Why they already have things missing!

And my Fresh-Air Mother was mad jealous . . .

FRESH-AIR MOTHER: (*Drunk Bette Davis:*) Well, little Johnny is a stuttering, masturbating, bedwetting, glue sniffing, little Latin loser (*chuggs*).

What a liar. I didn't stutter . . .

FRESH-AIR FATHER: Ignore the fucking drunk, Jesus. Did I tell you I love Mexican women. Is your mother single? I haven't had sex in a year.

It was so great to find out that white people were fucked up too. I'll always love my Fresh-Air family for giving me that. But then I had to go home which sucked cause we were poor but my father was cheap on top of that. It's a bad combo yo. He'd do anything not to give us presents and one X-mas eve he went to the reef . . .

POPS: Okay boys, stay right here. I'm going to try to save Santa. Cone esta suicidal. Ye ne se que va paser. (*Slam. Quivers with cold.*) Santa don't jump. (*Puff.*) Think of the children. (*Puff/teeth chatter.*) Pull yourself together man. He he. (*Scream.*) I'm sorry children Santa just killed himself. We won't be having Xmas this year. Instead we're going to read from the encyclopedia.

JOHN: You suck dad.

POPS: What? You don't know how good you got it. I was so poor thank God I was a boy or I wouldn't have had anything to play with. I hope you have children someday then you'll see. I put a curse on you. Sofrito cuchifrito que se joda un poquito.

MAKE THE WHITE PEE COME OUT

OR BOYS THAT WENT PEEP

But my father eventually gave me a present–a younger brother. Someone to torment. I called him Serg and he called me Master. And Serg and I shared the same bed and the same room until we went to college. And one night I had my father's encyclopedia open to naked natives of Mesoamerica . . .

SERG: Aw, come on, John, let me see Dad's encyclopedia!

JOHN: No way, man. They're still awake and besides when you see the pictures you're gonna make monkey noises!

SERG: I don't make monkey noises.

JOHN: Do too.

SERG: Do not.

JOHN: Oh yeah! Look!

(Serg makes monkey noise.)

SERG: Get back, I don't know how big this is gonna get. I'm gonna release the hostages, John! *(Monkey noises.)* OOOH!

(SFX: *Door opens. Kids snore hard.*)

POPS: I know you're not sleeping. Put it away, Serg, unless you want me to smack it and if I have to come back one more time it's gonna cost you years off your life and I'm not talking about the Medicaid ones at the end.

(SFX: *Door closes.*)

SERG: He's so powerful. John, he's like a superhero.

JOHN: *(Batman style.)* Yeah, right, whatever. Super Latin dad . . . yeah. Whip your ass *redder than Mars, Latin Dad/Can kick the door in the bathroom while you are beating off, Latin dad/Can't get mad at his boss so he takes it out on you, Latin dad/Puts the funk in dysfunctional/His kids are so rambunctional/He's my hero, he's my villain/He's Latin, Latin, Latin, Latin Daaaaaaaaaaaaad.*

(SFX: *Door opens.*)

POPS: So now you're making up songs about me? I'VE HAD IT WITH YOU TWO! If I hear one more peep out of you, you're gonna get a visit from the X-mas belt you made for me! And cardboard stings.

SERG: K'Dad!

JOHN: Sorry, Dad!

POPS: ONE MORE PEEP!

(SFX: *Door close.*)

JOHN: (*Beat:*) Peep. Peep. Pa-pa-peep.

SERG: Peep . . . peep . . . peee-pppee peep!

JOHN: Peeeeeeeeep. Peeeeeeeep.

(SFX: *Door opens. Whips SFX.*) . . .

POPS: Okay, that's it! I'm gonna spank the hell . . . No, you want
    me to hit you— you sick puppies. So instead, I'm gonna tell you
    a little bedtime story. (*Fast.*) Once a upon a time there were two
    boys from Queens / And an evil monster lived under their bed
    plotting schemes / They peeped and touched themselves with
    their fingas / And the monster came out and bit off their pingas.
    (*Maniacal laugh.* SFX: *Door closes.*)

We were paranoid so we stayed up and went through all 27 volumes
of that damned encyclopedia in one night.

MY PARENTS' DIVORCE

Which really wasn't a big deal cause my parents fighting kept us up most nights. Cause my parents had a funky relationship, man. They argued about everything and when they ran out of nasty things to say about each other they started in on each other's ancestors . . .

MOMS: (*Files nails:*) Your father comes from a long line of losers. In ancient Spain Leguizamo meant chamber pot emptier. Que conquistador y que mierda.

POPS: (*Reads newspaper, saws:*) Your mother's people were brown naked coked up savages. They didn't come on the boats they were so coked up they swam all the way.

And some day, I'm gonna have to tell my kids the real story and it's not gonna start . . . "Once upon time . . ." Cause that's for white fairy tales. Latin history starts, "You *motherfuckers* ain't never gonna believe this shit . . ." Aight cause not even the discovery channel knows our story. Spanish Europeans came over-sexed up the Indians, *menagetroised* it with some black folk. And one of those was my ancestor: loser Leguizamo. Who came to the New World, where a chamber pot emptier could front like a conquistador and met my great great great great great Incan princess who was a Latin honey like J-Lo. And she went to meet the boats . . .

INCAN PRINCESS GRANDMOTHER: Mm. Mm. Here comes a
   whiteboy with enough syphilis for two.

and loser disembarks on his horse (*gallops and whineys*) . . .

CONQUISTADOR GRANDFATHER: (*Gets off horse.*) Greetings
   brown heathen hairless savage. (*Sword out.*) I come to take your
   city of gold.

INCAN PRINCESS GRANDMOTHER: You can't take my bling bling.

CONQUISTADOR GRAMPS: I hear you sacrifice your virgins. Are
   you a virgin?

INCAN PRINCESS GRANDMOTHER: Does ass fucking count?

After fifteen years of arguing over our origins my parents finally agreed on something–divorce. It was a nasty divorce for everybody except my father cause my mother must have got her lawyer from Sesame Street . . .

LAWYER: (*Kermit voice:*) Mister Leguizamo listen to reason. Be a do
   be don't be a don't be. Scooby dooby do.

SINGLE MOM

So my pops got everything and my Mother got—us. And she got to be a single Mom, which is a polite way of saying, "broke-exhausted-and-nobody'll-date-your-ass." And she'd be in the kitchen cooking . . .

MOMS: Now I have to be both mother and father to you. I can't wait till you grow up and move out so I can party again.

JOHN: Why don't you let your mustache grow and I'll call you pops?

MOMS: Que Que. *That's it!* Dame my chancleta. Thank you. Now turn the radio up so the neighbors can't hear.

(*MUSIC: Break beat.*)

MOMS: Atrevido, baboso, mocoso, inutil. Sangano, condenado, syn-
verguenza, diablo.

JOHN: No, Mom. Ow. No Mom. Ow. No. Mom.

(*Scream "au" as I twirl up.*) And that's how Latin hip hop was born.

GRAMPS AND GRAMS

D*rinks water:*) Ah vodka! Then my Moms couldn't deal with my brother and I so she made me go live with my grandparents. And my Gramps was a very handsome man with a mane of white hair he looked like a Matinee Idol but when he lost his teeth he looked like an anus.

And when he got a stroke it moved to the side. And Gramps used to make me and my grandmother play poker with him every afternoon . . .

GRAMPS: Five card Chicago-low ball. Bet's on you Lulu. LULU!

GRAMS: (*Sews:*) Ay! You know Johnny, when I was a young girl, I wanted to marry a big somebody or nothing. So I got my wish. The first man that got me pregnant—I think? Give me one card.

GRAMPS: Let her talk, John, I don't care. Cause I'm gonna die soon.

Ha ha. I can't wait. Take me God. Please. Here's your card and dealer takes two. Papi?

JOHN: I'm sticking. Grampa, why don't you leave her?

GRAMPS: Because, mijo, the devil you know is better than the devil you don't know. Besides she's still great in bed. (*Sticks tongue out.*)

GRAMS: Ay que sangano. Where are they oh . . . yeah. (*Hikes up her tits and licks her lips.*) Deuces wild.

JOHN: Oh, please, you two, I don't want to know. La la la. I fold. I can't wait to grow up and get the hell out of this house.

GRAMPS: Why do you try so hard to be happy? Life isn't about smiling and fun it's about failure, pain, and Budweiser and it also helps to know you're gonna die soon. I can't wait. Haha.

BIRTH OF THE SEXAHOLIX/

RAPUNZEL GARCIA

I couldn't wait to get the hell out of that mad house and high school became my refuge. I was 16 which is 35 in Ghetto. And pretty soon all I could think about was females but all girls want are the ganstas, outlaws, the cool guys. So I wasn't getting any.

So I didn't get in. So I round up; English, Xerox, and Fucks Funny. And we started our own bad boy gang: the Sexaholix. And we'd serenade the hottest mamis in Queens. We once sang to this hot, hot girl whose father was a cop and who kept her locked up in their, third floor apartment. We called her Rapunzel Garcia. (*Climbs ladder:*) One night we broke into a parked elevated subway across her window and we grabbed the conductor's mic . . .

JOHN: (*Beat box:*) Hey, Rapunzel over here. Hit it Xerox.

Now what you're about to hear is no test / But we Sexaholix are the best / I saida, la-di-da-di we like to party / We'll sing and dance till you're goddamn sorry / Ha ha ha / I'm the Latin from Manhattan / Got more magic than Aladdin / Abra cadrabra I turn girl's legs to gelatin / Ha ha ha? / Fee to the Fie / Fo to the fum / Don't be mad cause your boy is hung like a . . . Hee haw hee haw! All you, Xerox.

XEROX: Yeah, yeah. Hee haw! Hee Haw!

ENGLISH: *A little coitus never hoiteded us.*

JOHN: (*Interrupts:*) OK that's enough . . . Yo, Rapunzel, how'd you like it?

RAPUNZEL: You guys are like so brave and funny.

JOHN: Well, come down.

RAPUNZEL: I can't because my father's on his way.

Next thing I know we're being cuffed and thrown in separate jail cells. (*Holds on to bars.*) And I was worried cause I was young, Latin, and friendly. In a cell with a bunch of degenerate freaks . . .

DEGENERATE: I'm a turn that ass out, boy!

And I knew I had to turn things around real quick before I'm celebrating my fiftieth anniversary as Lola the prison bitch. So I became the baddest, hardest punk alive . . .

JOHN: (*Pathetic attempt:*) Who's gonna be my bitch? I said who's gonna be my bitch? Somebody's gonna gonna suck my dick who's it gonna be?

MOM: John?!

JOHN: Mom?! How long you been listening?

MOM: (*On the verge of tears:*) Long enough, mijo, but whatever you and your bitches do is none of my business.

The arrest was good for me cause it got everybody's attention but Rapunzel's cause she thought she was better than me cause she was Argentinian and had no Indian or nothing in her . . . yet.

ESPERANZA AND WALTER/

RING THE BELL AND CHECK THE OIL

So I went to my Aunt Esperanza and Uncle Walter for some advice. They were the sexual pioneers of our family. Esperanza was a lesbian and Walter was gay and they just got together only to have a child BUT they weren't having any luck cause just the idea of having sex with Walter made Esperanza so nervous she stuttered.

ESPERANZA: (*Covers face:*) I'll teach how to make love a woman. It's all about the ppppe . . . dddeee . . . brbr . . . Just cccheck the oil and ring ttthe bbbell *(2x).*

WALTER: (*Pushes her aside:*) Ay, que asco! Casi me vomito! Please that image is so unnecessary. Women take forever. I still don't have any feeling in my face. Look, John, I don't repeat gossip, so listen good. Women take forever. I still have no feeling in my face. As soon I can give her a child I'm gonna go out and find me

Mr. Wrong and when I do I'm gonna bang him like a screen door during a hurricane. (SFX.) Ay me falta aire. Que escandalo.

JOHN: But I wanna know how to get Rapunzel?

WALTER: We're giving you choices, papi. This is America. (*Sings:*) Oh, Jose can you see? So you can do whatever you want and no one has a right to bother you except bisexuals they're just greedy. Pick a hole. You know what I mean. (*Snaps.*)

ESPERANZA: Look, I'll ggggive you a sure thing. Bbbring (*stutterfest*) her home and light candles; make it warm, give her wine and repeat everything she says back to her. Women love to hear themselves talk. Then you can grrr . . . sttt . . . prprpr . . . you can fuck her!

BLUE BALLS STRATEGY

I took Esperanza's advice: Warm, Booze, Repeat. But first I had to convince Rapunzel to go out with me so I bribed her . . .

RAPUNZEL: Where's the TV set you promised me? You said you were gonna give me your TV. Where is it?

JOHN: I said later. After the date. That was the deal.

(SFX: *Door.*) Espy said make it warm. I'll go one better. So I turned the thermostat to 90, oven to broil, and closed all the windows. And I turn around and Rapunzel is . . .

RAPUNZEL: (*Dehydratedly hangs onto stool:*) I can't breathe. Agua. Aguuuaaaaa. Help me somebody. Help me!

Espy said wine so I got us some vodka laced with scotch and whis-
key/gin (SFX: *Pours.*) . . .

JOHN: May the wind behind you never be yours.

RAPUNZEL: You are like so stupid. I like that. Cause I hate my life.
My father tells me Latin men are shit, awful, who are gonna disrespect me I should just have sex with you and show him.

Espy said repeat so I was like Xerox . . .

JOHN: (*Drink:*) Yes, have sex with me. I'm shit! You're father's right.
I'll try to disrespect you.

(*Rips jacket off. Drinks again. Hops*) Let me start by disrespecting your
breasts. Do you prefer left or right?

RAPUNZEL: (*Runs:*) See, you're not taking me seriously.

JOHN: You don't know how serious I am. Come on, baby. Let me
put the tip in. Okay, touch it then. Fuck, just look at it then.

RAPUNZEL: (*Eyes closed:*) No you're gonna go crazy on me.

JOHN: Oh baby, just do me or else the sperm'll turn back in on me
and poison me. It's a slow horrible death. You ever seen a brown
man with blue balls? They never go back.

RAPUNZEL: Alright. Mercy fuck. But you better not tell anybody.

I promise. So I whip it out . . . (Hops.)

RAPUNZEL: Oh my God, you're so . . . small.

JOHN: I like to think of it as your vagina's too big.

And she was like . . . (SFX: *Steps. Door.*)

COLLEGE HORNY DOG

So after a couple of years of giving girls all my appliances and not getting anything in return, I went to college and made up for lost time and had lots of wild meaningless sex. I was like a horny dog humping my way from class to class . . . "Hey, Bob, I failed philosophy. But I'm sure it was Nieztche who said: Der mensch ist was uber . . . Fuck, I'm late for psych. See ya at the beer blast." Down with apartheid. Working my way through college . . . "How would you like your burger sir, medium, well? Hold that thought. I'll be right back!"

E ventually, I got tired of meaningless sex. Yes, you can get tired of sex. There had to be more to life and my search for that something meaningful led me to this diner late one night, where I met this waitress slash actress. 40. Beautiful. Well meaning. Her name was Penny, a divorcee starting her life anew. Just like I was and we talked all night and in the morning she taught me everything . . .

PENNY: (*Gum-chewing New York Italian. Penny Marshall.*) Slower. Na higher . . . to the right. No my right. Okay wait, a little longer. Little longer.

And I'm like . . .

JOHN: Tangents, parabolas, Isosceles triangles. I don't think I can make it last longer, Penny.

Then I hear . . . (SFX: *Pussy fart.*)

JOHN: What was that?

PENNY: Nothing. Just a quiff. She's talking to you. She says you got
   a lot to learn.

So at twenty-one, I moved out of my grandparents' house and stopped
living off of them. Moved in with Penny and started living off her.
Her place was so small the furniture was painted on the walls. Sitting
down was a bitch. "No thanx I'll stand."

   It was just so exciting to be around Penny too and she was so good
to me. Dragged me to acting classes, made me read tons of books.
And she was so open. Took me to all kinds of Seminars, her favorite
was kareoke with a Japanese teacher Mr. Mihoko. (*Pull stand out, put
mic in.*) And she felt I had to keep improving my mind so she made
me go to feminist seminars and on the drive home she was mad inspired . . .

PENNY: (*Drives, traffic yells:*) I'm tired of being dominated by white
   male supremacist language and its phallocentric testosterona-
   cracy. You following me, John? Why menstruation, John? Why
   not womenstration. Why herpes? Why not himpes. Why diction-
   ary? Why not pussy-tionary.

And a few months go by and we're a couple sharing the bathroom
and I'm the happiest I've ever been and one morning, the unspeak-
able is spoken . . .

PENNY: (*Shaves her pit:*) Oh, John, these past three months have
   been so exciting. You make me feel young.

JOHN: (*Shaves:*) Penny, I never knew it could be this good. I've never felt like this. I la . . . la . . . I la . . .

PENNY: Is that a commitment I hear?

JOHN: (*Cuts himself:*) OW, I la . . . la . . .

PENNY: Oh, shit, John, I love you too.

ABORTION

T hen a year goes by and she keeps improving me because I'm never good enough for her. And one morning we're in the bathroom and she tells me she's pregnant and I was like . . .

JOHN: (*Shaves his pit:*) Wow! Wow! Are you sure it's yours?

PENNY: (*Plucks:*) Don't worry your pretty little head about it. I'm getting an abortion.

JOHN: Wait a minute. I have rights, you know. I mean, it's mine too. And it could be fun. Someone to tell what to do. Fetch things for me. Wow, the power. The control. I could really do some damage. We could be ourselves. They're gonna hate us anyway.

PENNY: You know you got a point. It's not fair to kill the fetus and let the father live. Bye, John.

(SFX: *Steps. Door.*) And she sent me packing. I was Gone.

And I should've said I loved her but I didn't have a clue what love felt like considering the family I came from. So I entered into the hell of post-breakup.

You know when you're alone in your room and time just slows down to a complete standstill . . . (*Slo-mo.*)

JOHN: Oh, my God. I'm so alone. What the fuck am I gonna do to-day? Isn't this day ever gonna end?

KARAOKE NIGHTMARE

nd then my father calls . . .

POPS: You feel confused and feeling unloved. Get used to it. As you go through life falling in love over and over again you learn that with women you have to be manly but have a feminine side. Be ying. Be yang. Be schizophrenic. You're a conquistador—get off the pity pot and join me for a drink. See you in half an hour.

And I get to this karaoke bar (*Cue*) and my Pops is there hitting on these two women who look like they're thirty—if you combine their ages . . .

POPS: Tell me about yourself, your dreams, your struggles, your telephone numbers? There he is. Hey, John, papi. Let me introduce you to my kid brother.

JOHN: I'm so glad to see you. I need to talk to you. Penny's here! With her Japanese boyfriend. I'm gonna have to go . . . Oh shit she's looking over here.

POPS: Go up, John, and sing for to her. Win her back.

JOHN: No, way. I have pride you know . . . (*Music kicks in.*) *I can't live if living is without you / I can't live. I can't give anymore* . . . That was horrible.

JOHN: (*Cont'd:*) You made me make an ass out of myself. I've never done that before, Dad.

POPS: Sure you have, Dad. We call each other "dad." It's this thing we have. (*Pushes him away.*)

JOHN: Look, she's kissing him. She doesn't love me anymore. It's over. Penny has somebody. You even have somebody . . . I'm . . . *(Mic-left hand) All by myself–I don't wanna be–all by myself anymore. . .*

POPS: I'll show you how's it done. (*Mic-right hand*) . . . *All by himself John doesn't want to be. All by himself he'll always because* (what's her name?) *Penny, you pussy whipped him.* (SFX) That's how you do it. I showed her.

JOHN: Thank you. She's leaving but thank you anyway. Penny! Stop! Wait. Give me a chance. I'll be anything you want me to be. I'll change. Look, Penny I'm . . . I'm *turning Japanese / I think I'm turning Japanese / I really think so.* Over here. Don't leave . . . *I'm turning Japanese / I think I'm turning Japanese / I really think so* . . . Penny, I la la la . . .

(*Runs. Black Out.*) (*"Turning Japanese" by The Vapors.*)

Intermission

*S*alsa music kicks in. John dances from the audience:) That's the heartbeat of all Latin people. (*Sits on the lip of the stage:*) And if you're off beat by this much (*example*) you're fucked for life.

And I was off beat for a while so decided to be alone. Figure myself out. Grow. And I pursued my career and got into my first movie–and was cut out of my first movie and my mom was . . .

MOMS: At least you were kind of subliminal.

And my Pops was . . .

POPS: I'd like to see you in a snuff picture.

"Thanks Dad." And while I was growing I met this hot, young, Latin actress . . .

EVELYN: How you doing? My name is Evelyn. And I couldn't help
noticing you were staring at my tits, right? (*Snorts:*) Shuddup.
Stop!

Ever date an Actress? Oh boy! . . .

EVELYN: John, tell me all about myself. You know, I was the one that
was gonna make it out. But you know what I got on my SATs?
I got nail polish. But I'm gonna make it, John. That's why I'm
thinking of changing my name to something white sounding.
How about just Visa? It could work right? Cause when I was born
I had blond hair and blue eyes and if you look at my eyes in the
right light they look hazel. Looky, looky, looky, look.

And I looked at Evelyn and there was no genetic-way-in-hell her DNA
would have given her hazel eyes except in her twisted self-hating Latin
brain. And this stupidity made me sad and this sadness made me la la
love her. I thought, I can save her. I thought I could pygmalionize her
the way Penny had molded me but with more sensitivity . . .

JOHN: Evelyn, because I like you just the way you are, I've drawn
up a ten-point program that will completely change you for the
better.

EVELYN: Oh, my God, what are all these pie charts?

JOHN: Kinko's is amazing, isn't it? Okay, now pay attention . . .
Number one . . . lower your voice to a sexy rasp because your
high pitch only bats can hear. Two: lose the high heels it makes
me look taller. Three: 1985 called and they want their music back.

Okay, I was drunk with power. I admit it. But eventually, every creation must kill its creator and my sweet Latin thing turns into girl-friendstein . . .

EVELYN: Yeah, Kinko's is amazing, motherfucker. Now, turn your pie chart to page three right after it says you're not my goddamn father. Now, did you know food tastes better when you chew with your mouth closed? And *Super Mario Brothers* sucked. And why can't you stand up for me in front of your moms? Is it cause you're still attached to her umbilical cord or is that her dick?

JOHN: (*Stays on floor.*) Don't you ever talk about my mother's . . . dick that way.

EVELYN: You know why I don't get wet anymore? Cause your putting me down doesn't turn me on anymore.

JOHN: Well, as long as I can spit.

EVELYN: Oh, my god! (*Undoes blouse and unstraps bra.* SFX: *Ping!*) No real man could say something like that. I don't even know if you're man enough anymore . . .

JOHN: (*Undoing pants:*) I'll show you . . . who's not man enough! Is this–man–enough . . .

EVELYN: Ay!–Ay!–Ay! Que Animal!

And somewhere between our first fight and this brawl I managed to discover something magical. The bigger the fight the better the sex and life became a beautiful living hell. And so, we did what some couples do when they have conflicts they can't possibly resolve: we got married.

MARRIAGE

I can remember "when" and "where," I just can't remember exactly "why" cause my friends got me so stinking drunk the night of my bachelor party . . .

FUCKS FUNNY: (*Toasts:*) Here's to Latin women. They're like blowup dolls, put a ring on their fingers and poof their hips expand.

XEROX: (*Drinks:*) Oh, shit! poof. That's cold. Poof.

JOHN: Come on, fellas, you got married. There's gotta be something good about marriage right?

FUCKS FUNNY: (*Laughs:*) Yeah, makes your life seem longer. I've been married to Cuca for only a year but it feels like forever, dog. Look, player, this is from the heart. If you and Evelyn last more than six months, I'll blow Xerox.

XEROX: Yeah, yeah, blow me. Yeah.

But I didn't listen to the fellas cause I thought they were jealous cause I was the last to get married. So I had my nuptuals in Vegas at the Elvis Chapel. And a year later Evelyn and I were celebrating our first anniversary . . .

JOHN: (*Humps like jockey:*) Could you move a little?

EVELYN: (*Bites her nails:*) I told you I'm not in the mood.

JOHN: But even people who don't fuck–fuck on their anniversary.

EVELYN: (*Flips page:*) Now, look what you did. You made me lose my place in the book.

JOHN: But baby, can't you at least fake it?

EVELYN: What do you think I've been doing?

JOHN: Well, then you suck as an actress.

EVELYN: Maybe, if I had a bigger part.

(*Turns page.*)

THE ALCOHOLIX/

MY DIVORCE

T hank you. So the last of the "sexaholix" joined the "alco-holix" and I was staying out late nights with my friends never wanting to come home . . .

JOHN: (*Drunk as hell:*) *Break up to make up. That's all we do.*

ENGLISH: *First you lovededed me then you hatededed me.*

JOHN: Shh. Don't wake up the monster.

EVELYN: It's too late. I'm already up.

JOHN: Don't hit me. My friends were just leaving. (*To fellas:*) Don't go.

FRIENDS: See ya! See ya. Yeah yeah later. (SFX: *Wind.*)

EVELYN: Good, fine, we were only supposed to go to my parents' anniversary tonight but that's okay you hang out with your friends cause I'mma just gonna sew up my pussy so you can't fuck me anymore and then you'll dick'll wither and fall off and then you'll have pussy and then maybe your friends'll wanna fuck you.

She really said that. I couldn't write a line like that . . .

EVELYN: That's it. I'm leaving. You make my life miserable! (*Undoes blouse*.) Oh, John, I know you're not man enough to try to make it work out one more time.

JOHN: I'll show you who's not man enough? Is this (*humps*) man (*humps*) enu . . . (*Sexes her up but goes out cold*.)

EVELYN: John, John, wake up. I want a divorce.

JOHN: Divorce? But you're supposed to love me no matter what.

EVELYN: You must be confusing me for Jesus.

(SFX: *Footsteps. Door.*) And she was gone. I don't know why the divorce came to me as such a big surprise? All Leguizamos grow up, get married, start a family, fail, get divorced, end up alone and miserable. So I was right on track . . .

GRAMPA'S PINGA

I was broke and depressed but not as depressed as when I had to move back in with my grandparents.

(*Stands by stool:*) And I was depressed but not as depressed as when I had to move back in with my grandparents. Oh, yeah! And my grandfather's health had really deteriorated but he didn't suffer from senility. He kind of enjoyed it . . .

GRAMPS: (*Kicks feet:*) Help! Help! I fell in the toilet.

GRAMS: How the hell did you come to fall in?

GRAMPS: I didn't come to fall in. I came to take a shit.

And then my Grama turns Gramps over to me. She was fine to torture him when he was healthy but now that he was suffering on his own, she decided to study the bible and cram for her finals. And I became his full-time caregiver, which meant I had to help him with all his daily activities and I do mean all . . .

GRAMPS: John, papi, take me into my office.

JOHN: (*Escorts Gramps:*) Okay, look, Gramps, I'll help you on to the toilet but you gotta do the rest yourself. What? I have to hold it for you? Alright . . . (*Holds pinga:*) You're spraying everywhere. What are you a little fire truck? How the fuck did I get this job?

So there I am a grown man, divorced and depressed, holding my Grampa's *pinga. And he's still scheming* . . .

GRAMPS: (*Sits:*) John, Papi, help me escape. Look, I've saved up enough money for a cab. To anywhere–how about Hawaii. (*Looks at his weeny:*) Shake it. You and I both know you're not happy. Come on, I got girls for both of us. What do you say?

(*Holds his heart. Sings:*) Sing with me . . . *The Jordan river's deep and wide but soon I'll see the other side* . . . I'm afraid. Hold my hand.

JOHN: It's okay, Grandpa. Don't worry. I'm here.

GRAMPS: Oh, that's nice. But who are you?

My Grandpa finally got his wish to escape and I just stayed in my room for a couple of days because it was the first time in my life somebody I loved died–and it was too much.

HIGH AT GRAMPS'S FUNERAL

B ut on the day of his funeral my friends had the brilliant idea of giving me something to numb the pain . . . (*Stand-up.*)

ENGLISH: Here, smokeded this. It's the only way I can dealeded with this messeded up world.

JOHN: English, I'm not getting high for my grandpa's funeral.

FUCKS FUNNY: Dude, I'm telling you you're gonna need it. My Grams died last year. Look, it makes the church music sound like the Beatles and the munchies helps choke down the communion wafer. If you know what I'm saying?

XEROX: Yeah. Yeah. Beatles, munchies, etc., John.

JOHN: Okay, if you think it's gonna help. (*Beat.*) Alright I didn't realize how down I was.

(*Small toke. Bigger toke:*) And I started feeling nice and detached and philosophical even. "Death is life's way of saying. Slow down. You've done too much." Life spelled backwards is "efil." (*Gestures: Whatever that means?*) Until I get to the funeral parlor and I realize (*pause*) I've made a huge mistake. Cause now I was mad paranoid. (*Freaks out.*) I kept thinking everybody's thinking I did it . . .

JOHN: I didn't do it. Why would I do it? I'm the only one who would hold his pinga.

And we had an open casket. (SFX: *Open casket.*) Cause you know how we Latin Catholics are, we don't trust them to give us our dead; we wanna make goddamn sure.

And there was my grandfather, all stern from the rigor mortis and he had too much make up on he looked like a Latin Reagan. And my Mother throws herself on the body . . .

MOMS: Porque, dios. Porque? Why take him? Take my mother.

I watch as they drag my mom away and I look back at my cabaret-looking Gramps. And all of a sudden I get pot lip. And I'm sad but everybody's thinking I'm smiling. I start crying but everybody's thinking I'm laughing. (*Laughs and cries.*) And my Grama comes up to me . . .

GRAMS: Take that stupid smile off your face and show some respect, descarado!

And she bends over the coffin and kisses him with her eyes open cause she still didn't trust him . . .

GRAMS: I know you're not dead, pendejo. Who do you think you're fooling, desgraciado? You think you can escape me? But I'm coming soon to make your life miserable forever. (*Head down.*) Cause I don't think I can make it without you.

She must of held it in for fifty years cause she let out a cry. A cry that had never been used . . . (*Small cry. Two beats of crying. Nothing.*) And nothing came out. And then I thought I could hear my Grandfather talking to me . . .

GRAMPS: John, papi! Psst. Down here.

JOHN: Gramps?

GRAMPS: John, papi, life is simple; never fall in love with a woman that kisses with her eyes open cause you can see right to their heart. Oye, hey, hey, don't look so sad, what, I know, you want me to be there so we can play. Hey, remember all the times I took you fishing to the pet shop. That look on your face made me very happy. Kids are angels even the bad ones like you. Just gotta give them roots and wings. *Oye*, I got an idea. Take my ashes and put them in an etch-a-sketch. So you can play with me whenever you want.

THE MOTHER OF MY KIDS

t took a long time for my grandfather's advice to sink in. I'm a stubborn guy and I gotta make my own mistakes. And I was making plenty of them. I had hit thirty and I didn't want to end up like some old cheesy guy with a fat gut, bad hair plugs, and a leopard thong picking up women in dive bars . . .

JOHN: Hey, be different say yes.

So I became a workaholic and while I was working on a movie that should've gone straight to video I met Teeny, this hot pixie blond, who was everything I wasn't. Grounded, sane, and wasn't an actor. So I went for it. Finally I camped outside her apartment through rain and snow in one of those half-phone booths so my hair was dry but my pants looked like I'd peed in them and it worked. She brought me in and kissed me with her eyes closed. Then she read me the rules

. . .

TEENY: Look, before we get serious. I want you to know all about me. I'm very practical. I'm a Jew—I don't want anything from you that I can't return cause I've worked hard on myself so you don't have to. And if you could just be there for me sometimes when I need you—then we're golden. Let's play it by ear. Whatever happens, happens. Okay? Have fun. Go. (*Kisses.*)

And I applauded too. Teeny was amazing. So, I was tough on myself to mature and when my therapist said, "Congratulations emotionally you're now twelve years old. Thirteen here we come." So I knew I was ready to make love to her for the first time. Well, at least I thought I was . . .

JOHN: Hey, I'm sorry. This never happens to me. I must be kinky, I don't know, I can't get it up unless you treat me like shit.

TEENY: Okay, fuck you. Hey, we can do other things or not. You wanna talk. Okay let's talk. What do you wanna talk about? I know, tell me about your family.

JOHN: (*Cagey:*) They're fine thank you.

TEENY: Oh you're lucky. Cause my mother told my father the other day that I was a failure. And I asked her, "Why would you say something like that?" And she said, "I didn't know it was a secret."

JOHN: Oh, my God. You're damaged too.

TEENY: But at least I'm in therapy.

JOHN: I need more therapy. My brother used to make monkey noises when he masturbated.

TEENY: Oh, my God, that's so weird my cousin used to bleat like a
sheep.

JOHN: Hey, we're soulmates.

TEENY: Yeah, I don't want to marry you either.

JOHN: I la . . . la . . . la . . .

TEENY: (*Sweet:*) John . . . grow up.

And believe me I wanted to, cause, my God, a woman who calls me
on my bullshit and is sweet when she does it! What the fuck happened?! Did God give me a coupon!?

And the rest of that night was pillow talk. We hooked up and everything was going just right and about a year later we had our families meet at an X-mas party.

Don't worry I made everybody come in costume cause I wanted as many layers of camouflage on my family as possible. And my mother comes in dressed all orange and fishy smelling . . .

MOMS: Hello, everybody. Merry Navidad. Feliz X-mas.

JOHN: Mom, what the hell are you wearing?

MOMS: I'm Lox. Smoked salmon.

JOHN: Mom, go home and change.

MOMS: Oh, relax, I was only trying to impress. John, just help me on my schmear it's getting chilly all of a sudden.

And we lit Chanukah candles for Teeny's parents and my father blew them out . . .

JOHN: Dad, what the hell are you doing?

POPS: I thought it was my birthday.

JOHN: You people are embarrassing the hell out of me. Why can't you be like her parents?

And her father comes over . . .

TEENY'S DAD: Hey, Jorge, I wanna show you these photos. We just came back from Cancún. Boy do we love Mexico.

JOHN: No offense, sir but I'm not Mexican.

TEENY'S DAD: So, Jose, what part of Mexico did you say you were from?

JOHN: I didn't say it, cause I'm not Mexican.

TEENY'S DAD: Whatever. My daughter tells me that she loves you. You got my blessing.

JOHN: Pues orale, vato cholo.

What a perfect match. Her family was as messed up as mine.

A nd then she moved in with me, which freaked me out since I was sure she was gonna see me for who I really am: a self-absorbed, insecure, egomaniacal sexaholic actor–I wanted love but sometimes it's the scariest shit. (I needed a psychological enema.) So I resisted every bit of the way but at least we never went to bed mad; nope we stayed up and fought–so four days later . . .

JOHN: (*Nods out:*) Ow, what is that? Okay I'm awake.

TEENY: No you watch it. Do you know how angry I am? I could kill you. I could gouge out your eyes. I could eat your flesh.

JOHN: All I asked was if you have ever made love to another woman. What's the big deal?

TEENY: Why don't you work on satisfying one woman and then we'll graduate. What do you keep running away from?

JOHN: (*Yawns:*) I'm at a crossroads. How many times does man come to a crossroads?

TEENY: If they're like you. About every three months. Stop it John. Just be yourself that's all I want. That and kids.

JOHN: Kids? We don't need kids. We got me.

TEENY: John, I want to do this with you but my clock is ticking.

JOHN: Maybe you can put it on snooze.

TEENY: Not everything is a joke.

JOHN: Look, I'm sorry, your clock may be telling you to have children but mine is telling me to go to sleep. Good night. Oh, forget it. I can't sleep. I'm gonna walk it off.

So I went to my friends . . .

JOHN: Yo, fellas, Teeny wants kids. You got 'em; I mean, what's it like?

ENGLISH: My kids have taughteded me alot. Taughteded me, how I don't speakeded so good.

XEROX: Yeah. Yeah. Kids are great just never raise your hand to them. It leaves you open to a shot in the midsection.

FUCKS FUNNY: My daughter just learned how to talk dog. Now we don't know how to teach her how to shuddup. Word, just this morning she told the teacher at school, "My daddy brushes my mommy's teeth with his pee pee."

"Thanx fellas." The guys meant well but maybe I was going to have to figure this fathering thing on my own.

mean, I'd lived my whole life for myself by myself and I survived all the Fresh-Air Fund mothers, dead santas and Grampa's pingas and maybe it was a sign that it was time to give something back. And I'm not my father, I'm not gonna be my parents and there's a chance I might be good or at least different. (So I talked myself into it.) So I decided to go for it but when I went to tell Teeny the great news . . .

TEENY: Oh, that's wonderful. Cause I'm already pregnant. Now excuse while I go throw up.

SONOGRAMS

All of a sudden I wasn't so sure again but we went for it anyway cause SHE WAS SO FAR along. But like every guy I was gender specific. I wanted a boy. Cause you feel you relate easier passing down your dysfunction. So when we went for our first sonogram, I was in mad denial and we had a Korean doctor and he was like . . .

DR. KOREAN: I'm telling you it's a girl. It's a girl! For the millionth time no ding dong! Get out of my office.

THE BIRTH

So we had a home birth. (*Put mike on stand.*) And Teeny got a Brazilian wax cause she knew I was gonna videotape it. And I'm videotaping. And she's squatting. (SFX: *Camera.*) And I'm watching my favorite safe haven being ripped open by this eight-pound object. And all I can think is—damn! Next time we have sex I'm gonna have to bang the hell out of the sides for her to feel me at all.

And I was still hoping for a boy and I'm like . . .

JOHN: B to the O to the Y . . .

And the head pops out and back in . . .

JOHN: Look, Teeny, it's got the face of a boy. It's a boy.

. . . And the shoulder pops out and then . . .

JOHN: It's a boy and what a goddamn boy!

And the midwife says . . .

MIDWIFE: Ah that's the umbilical cord.

JOHN: I knew that. Honey, keep pushing. Make rude noises. Oh,
here it comes. Here he comes. What? You want me to catch him?
I'm no Jorge Posada. Push. (*Big moment of catching. Looks for
pinga.*) It's a . . . girl.

And she's all hot and gooey . . .

JOHN: You want me to cut the umbilical cord. If I'm doing all the
work why the fuck am I paying you?

And you gotta wait for it to finish pulsing. (SFX: *Heartbeat.*) And it's
like a telephone cable, "Goddamn-son-of-a-bitch! Could you help
me?" And I cut it and I hold her in my arms and she was so present.
She stared back at me and I fell in love with her right then and there.
And I had a moment of clarity. No matter what I do I'm gonna fuck
her up.

I place her on Teeny's breast and she starts suckling right away.
(*Nursing.*) It's the most beautiful thing I ever saw.

Now I have a confession to make. I didn't breast feed as a child so
now I want to all the time. And I'm pushing boogie out of the way . . .

JOHN: Come on, let your daddy at it. Hey, you got me in the eye. It's
kind of sweet and salty at the same time. Just like semen. (*Beat.
Looks around.*) Or so I HEAR! Hypocrites.

IT'S GOT A DING DONG

Just when we were learning to manage our lives: Boogie was sleeping through the night, I was getting a little sex. Just when we had it all figured out, Teeny tells me she's pregnant again. We go back to the Korean doctor . . .

KOREAN DOCTOR: Yes, it's got a ding dong. Jesus Christ, man. Get off my back.

Succeed where I failed. Win where I lost. And this time in the home birth I was a pro. I ordered Chinese food, I'm eating and telling the midwife what to do . . .

JOHN: (*Eats:*) Hey, Doc, I see the head crowning. She's dilated at least to eight centimeters. I think you should induce. Pass me the soy thank you very much.

And the second kid is a lot faster. It just pops the head out once or twice if you're lucky . . . (*One face pops out then flies out.*) Fuacata! And I caught him. Fdunk! (*Casual catch.*)

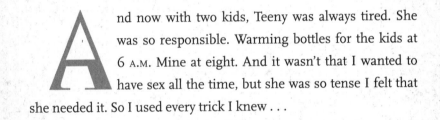

SECOND FIGHT

And now with two kids, Teeny was always tired. She was so responsible. Warming bottles for the kids at 6 A.M. Mine at eight. And it wasn't that I wanted to have sex all the time, but she was so tense I felt that she needed it. So I used every trick I knew . . .

JOHN: Here, I brought you aspirin.

SHE: But I don't have a headache.

JOHN: Ah ha.

SHE: Damn. But John, I've been with the kids all day. Alright, hurry, before they wake up.

I don't mind being hurried. It saves me the embarrassment of apologizing later . . .

JOHN: (*Whispers:*) Come on, Teeny, you gotta get into it.

SHE: But the baby is looking right at me.

JOHN: Pretend he's blind.

SHE: Oh, that's so sad. Now, I can't anymore. I'm sorry.

JOHN: Now I'm starting to feel like I'm getting replaced around here. Like I'm number two.

TEENY: No you're not. You're number three. I'm number two. It'll go back to normal.

JOHN: You said that three years ago. Okay, fine. I'm gonna go out and hang with my friends.

TEENY: John, grow up. You're always going somewhere. Why don't you stay home and watch Little Man and get to know him and let me and Boogie have a girl's night out.

JOHN: What a great idea—we'll all go.

TEENY: Don't wait up, John.

JOHN: Teeny, you know how I feel about you?

TEENY: Don't worry. I know you luh-luh-luh me.

(SFX: *Footsteps. Door.*)

COLICKY SON

And she leaves with Boogie. It wasn't like all the other times women had walked out on me. This time it was different. I wasn't crushed, I had a little hostage . . .

JOHN: Hey, Little Man. We're two guys alone together for the first time, Little Man. We'll watch a little TV, have pizza. Here, have some beer.

And the little prick gets colicky on me and cries one of those piercing screams that make you wanna rip out your ears. (*Screams.*) . . .

JOHN: Holy shit! What the hell do you want? I gave you food. We shared my milk. I know you can't talk but what the fuck do you want?

(*Baby silent screams like a puppet.*) And then I started to think he was doing it on purpose, competing with me . . .

JOHN: You think you can take me don't you? I know you're trying to take Teeny away from me. I see how you put your arm around her when you breast feed. Don't think I haven't noticed.

And he gives me back the same shifty-I-grew-up-in-New-York-City-too-motherfucker look that I have.

JOHN: Wait till you've got children you'll see. I put a curse on you. Sofrito cuchifrito que se joda un poquito. (*Screams.*) I start to freak out and I call the only other person who's been in this mess before . . .

POPS: Put 'im down and get out. Close the door. Okay, now break open a bottle. Not for him for you and check on him in two hours. So now you're finally beginning to appreciate all my hard work. You're lucky I was your father, cause I was never my father's favorite and I was an only child. My father was scared of his father and I was scared of my father and I wanted the same for you but today kids talk back to you before you get a chance to say anything. So you gotta kick ass from the start or they'll ruin your life, take your dreams, and just wreck your peace. Oh, Jesus Christ, I hated you Johnny. I hated you and loved you and wanted to kill you. You son of a bitch. I love you. Call any time. Bye.

My pops, the king of mixed feelings, going through male menopause.

nd evening comes and Teeny and Boogie still haven't shown up. And I'm afraid someone's gonna have to put Little Man to bed and I was afraid it was gonna be me. (*Opens door. Baby screams. Slams door.*) He's still alive. (*Walks away. Reconsiders.*) Oh, what am I afraid of? There's an angel in there–somewhere. Just gotta give him roots and wings right? Yeah right.

(SFX: *Opens door.*)

(*Lights dim.*)

JOHN: (*Screams.*) Shh! (*Screams.*) Okay, hey, Little Man, you feeling any better? Don't worry. Can I tell you a bedtime story? Alright, now you little sucker ain't never gonna believe this but . . . back in the day there was this man who grew up surrounded by monsters. (*Growls. Screams.*) Okay, I'm sorry. So he tried to run from them all his life but no matter how far he ran he couldn't escape the monsters. So he had to tame them. And when he did, he felt ready to have two little ones of his own. And he protected them as long as he could but then he had to let go because it was their turn to tame their monsters. And you will and you'll win. Cause I love you. I'm Superlatin Dad. Now here, play with your great-grandfather for a little while longer. I don't wanna hear a peep. Not one peep!

And I close the door . . . (SFX: *Closes door.*) . . . and I hear him say his first word . . . peep pa-peeeeeep! (*Black out.*)

This isn't "the end." It's the beginning.

ACKNOWLEDGMENTS

From *Freak*

A very special thank you to Dave Bar Katz whose immense contribution and vision really helped this show come to life, especially when I was ready to quit; Justine Maurer, my cutie pie, who sacrificed many hours to my mistress, my art, and who encouraged me onward; much gratitude to my mother, Luz, and my brother Sergio for their patience and understanding and above all their forgiveness for letting me expose dirty laundry, cause God knows I wouldn't have allowed this to happen if the roles were reversed; to Aury Wallington for all her hard work, making all the details happen so the sum could be whole; to Dennis Brooks for all his help; Mike Carroll for more help; to Julie Merberg whose idea was this very book and whose hard work made it happen. To Gena Merberg who took some great shots for us; to Johnny and Hilary Reinis who believed in us and produced a very successful run in San Francisco; Mark Russell at P.S. 122 for his constant support in every theatrical venture I've ever taken; Dave Lewis at Lower East Side Films; William Morris Agency, especially Scott Lambert, Brian Gersh, George Lane, Mike August, Clint

Mitchell, James Dixon; my manager Tom Chestaro for coming in and tying all the knots; and last but the most important, all my supportive and forgiving friends who sat there through countless, indulgent readings and to the nameless fans who did the same–thanks y'all.

—JOHN LEGUIZAMO

Special thanks to: John Leguizamo, for everything, but especially for letting me rip painful memories out of his head like so many rotten teeth and then being OK about trying to make it funny. To Julie "Nappy" Merberg, who sacrificed many hours to my mistress, John Leguizamo, and whose support and work are responsible for this book and so much else. Mom, Drew, Dad, Susan, Doug, Bisi, Jessica, Zach, and my Nans for family stuff to draw upon; Will Potter, Todd Owens, John Watkins, Seth Burns, Michael Robin for politely laughing through the horror of early readings; to Fausto for the use of his name; Gregory Mosher, for passion and a desire to return to a 5/1 ratio; and Mary South, for making *Freak* a book and taking a leap of faith based on an early reading to a hostile crowd. Also Mark Russell at P.S. 122, for providing a nurturing space, Jonathan and Hillary Reinis at Theatre on the Square, David Lewis, Jason Sloane, Kathy DeMarco, Aury Wallington, and Gena Merberg for helping with too many things to list that made the show happen. Thanks!

—DAVID BAR KATZ

From *Spic-O-Rama*

A real special SHOUT goes to Peter Askin and to the usual suspects for the usual crimes: Michael Bregman; David Lewis; Luz Leguizamo; Michael Robin; Theresa Tetley; Marshall Purdy; Philip Rinaldi; Lapacazo Sandoval; Sergio Leguizamo; Mark Russell of P.S. 122; Randy Rollison of H.O.M.E. for Contemporary Theatre and Art; the Goodman's Robert Falls, Roche Schulfer, and staff; the Gas Station's Osvaldo Gomariz;

Ellie Kovan of Dixon Place; the Public's George C. Wolfe; Chauncey Street Productions; Albie Hecht; Magda Liolis; John Hazard; Johnny Ray; Terry Byrne, Rick Shrout, and the staff at Westside Theatre–you know who you are; David Klingman; Samantha Mathis; Linda Gross; Gina Velasquez Healy; Steven Vause; John Vicey; Caroline Strauss; Brigitte Potter; Chris Albrecht; Bob Levinson; Tom Hansen; Suzanne Gluck; and my loyal friend David Bar Katz.

From *Mambo Mouth*

Mucho special thanx goes out to: Peter Askin, for being such a talented bud; Wynn Handman, for being a national treasure; David Rothenberg, for believing; Luz M. Leguizamo, for putting up with me; Sergio Leguizamo, for giving in to; Michael Bregman, for sticking up for; David Lewis, for figuring out how to; Theresa Tetley, for congeniality while under pressure; Island Records, for financing; and a special shout goes out to: Liz Heller; Mark Groubert; David Klingman; David B. Richards; Stephen Holden; Laurie Stone; Gina Velasquez Healy; Linda Gross; Juliet Wentworth; Judy Yip; Kim Merrill Askin, for giving up her honeymoon; Carolyn McDermott for letting me be crazy; Randy Rollison, H.O.M.E. for Contemporary Theatre; Mark Russell, P.S. 122; Mirtha Gregory; Angelo Parra, Jr.; Lapacazo Sandoval; Kate Lanier; Charlotte Rapisarda; Kevin Gregory; Angela Rodriguez; Dixon Place; Garage; Max Ferra, INTAR; Marshall Purdy; Michael Robin; Joe Onorato; Jeffrey Arsenault; Roxanne Laha; David Hughes; Eric Leonard; and friends, and friends of friends who sat through long, slow, unfunny, and uncatered evenings with no air-conditioning and many an insistence from me that "Hey, it will work. Shut up! I know what I'm doing. If you don't think so then you write it."

Peace.

CREDITS AND PERMISSIONS

From *Mambo Mouth*

BOOKS BY JOHN LEGUIZAMO

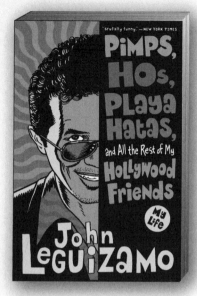

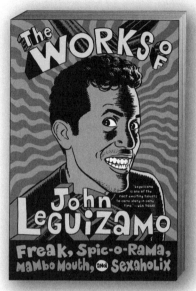

PIMPS, HOS, PLAYA HATAS, AND ALL THE REST OF MY HOLLYWOOD FRIENDS
My Life

ISBN 978-0-06-052072-4 (paperback)

"Leguizamo is one of the most exciting
talents to come along in some time."
—*USA Today*

"Candid yet searing. . . . Whether he
is being tough on Latin stereotypes or
describing his sexual conquests, the
text is hilarious—propelled by jokes,
quips and situations. . . . This mix
of the glib and the sometimes glam
presents a refreshing cultural tonic."
—*Publishers Weekly*

THE WORKS OF JOHN LEGUIZAMO
Freak, Spic-o-Rama, Mambo Mouth,
and *Sexaholix*

ISBN 978-0-06-052070-0 (paperback)

For the first time all in one volume, the
collected works of the renowned artist,
including *Freak, Spic-o-Rama, Mambo
Mouth*, and the never-before-published
Sexaholix—based on the sold-out
national tour of *John Leguizamo Live!*

"[Leguizamo is] a remarkably mature
writer. . . . Astonishing."
—*Newsweek*

"Brutally funny."
—*New York Times*